Whispers Through the Pines

Whispers Through the Pines

Kendal Lou Dickson

CONTENTS

This book is dedicated to my first true love, Lil Rico. You were the best dog and I will never forget all those times you sat beside me while I wrote. I wish you were here to see this.

Chapter 1

Spring is in full bloom. The pine trees are full and green, decorated with dainty little pine cones. A breeze carries the wildflowers' soft scent of pollen from the outskirts of Pine Valley throughout the entire town. Pine Valley is a secluded village that is encased by miles and miles of pine trees. There are some nearby mountains to the east and a river that runs parallel to the main road making the area a perfect habitat for wildlife. Some wolves, a large population of coyotes, mountain lions and a few bears roam around the area. Bears are rarely encountered, but if one is seen a farmer will usually set out a trap. When their livestock is their livelihood, they cannot take any chances.

Finding herself with some free time, one of the villagers, May Ferrothorn, decides to take her horse out for a ride on the outskirts of the town. The twenty-two-year-old is attired in a faded, blue shirt and white cotton pants. Her laced shoes are scuffed and dull from years of use. The sunlight kisses her lightly freckled face. Her long, dirty blonde hair is tied back in a braid. The wind catches the loose stands, pushing them back from her face.

May's horse, Red, is a sorrel gelding. His back is swaying from old age, hip bone protruding, and his once-shiny coat is dull. May has grown up on the back of this horse. He was always there to lend an ear to her troubles and offer her temporary escape from her abusive father. Even in old age, she still loves this horse more than anything.

The area is lightly wooded, its grass is uncut, at least four feet tall as it's slightly above the horse's hocks. Birds are chirping overhead, and rabbits are squeaking as they flee from the horse's heavy hooves. They walk slowly over the hills that they once practically flew over. She feels a calmness surround her.

Without warning, she hears a crunch and feels her horse falling out from underneath her. Everything happens in slow motion as she falls to the side of the saddle and onto the dirt hiding under the unruly grass, her head barely missing being slammed into a large rock. The world is spinning as she sits up and looks towards Red. He's struggling to get up, crying out pitiful whinnies, and panicking as his front right leg refuses to listen. Snapping back into reality May stands up to see what is trapping her mount. Her mouth gapes and a cold sweat perspires onto her skin. Red has stepped into a bear trap.

This rusty trap could have been placed by anyone as it's on the outskirt of town and not near any particular farm or household, perhaps even a weary traveler could have placed it when they spent the night before journeying into the town itself. Regardless, the grass prevented her from seeing it.

Blood is gushing from his pastern where the trap is embedded. Maybe it's naivety, maybe it's the shock from the fall, but all May can think is that she has to go find help for him. She starts running back towards the way they had ventured from calling out as loudly as she can.

"Somebody please help! Help me! My horse is hurt!"

May's legs begin to throb as her pace quickens. The farther she runs the harder it is for her to breathe due to her screaming and inability to breathe out of her nose while doing so. It seems like it is an eternity of running and shouting until she finally has a response.

"Hang on. I'm coming," a man says.

May stops in her tracks. Out of the woods adjacent to the town comes a black-haired man, riding a grey dappled horse with a dark mane and tail. The horse and rider approach her. The man extends his hand. Without a second thought, May grabs it as he rides by. He pulls her up behind him and she wraps her arms around his waist.

"Where's your horse? What's wrong with him?" he asks.

In vain, May cannot respond. Her throat is dry and swollen from all her shouting. Weakly she throws her arm by his shoulder, pointing in the northern direction she ran from.

"All right, hold on," he says.

He lifts his rein, pointing the horse's nose and adjusting their path. May squeezes her arms around him. She holds her head against his shoulder as he leans forward. Heat is radiating from the man, making May feel somewhat safe, secure. The grey mare runs harder. The horse has long strides. Each step consumes the ground in great lengths. By the time they reach

Red, May has been away from her horse for almost an hour now. Red is no longer panicking, he's just lying there as if he has accepted his inevitable fate. May slides off the back of the grey, while the man dismounts. They approach her horse. It's too late. Blood is dripping from Red's nostrils as he nickers quietly at her familiar face.

"It's okay old boy," May says.

She bends down next to him, stroking his neck. A few tears slip down her cheeks. Without a word, the man takes one look at Red and walks back to his horse who is impatiently snorting and pawing at the ground. He then walks back over to May and Red, holding a pistol in his hand. Her heart sinks, seeing the tarnished silver weapon.

"There is nothing else I can do," the stranger says.

"What? Can't you at least try?"

"Look at him."

She looks at Red. His hair is curled from sweating, fighting as he draws each quick breath. More tears slide down her cheeks. Nausea plagues her stomach. It feels like a balloon is inside her, growing and growing with no room.

"I know this is hard, but he's suffering, it's the kindest thing you or I could do for him," he says.

"O-okay..."

He lets out a deep sigh. Sadness haunts his face. She collapses against Red, pressing her cheek against his neck. Her fingers are entwined in his mane. She flinches as the stranger pulls the trigger. The air around them is briefly quiet, before it's replaced by the ringing in their ears. The stranger puts his hand on May's shoulder, lightly squeezing it, and kneels down next Red. After a few minutes, she's able to pull her head up. Her green eyes are red and puffy. She looks to the stranger, who is stroking Red's cheek and whispering something ineligible. It's intriguing to see a man be so kind and gentle to a horse he does not know.

She hasn't really paid much attention to his appearance until now. The stranger has a tan chiseled face with a cleft chin. His curly hair is a dark black, the length falls past his ears. He must have felt her staring, he looks up and their eyes lock. His eyes are a piercing bright blue that freeze her right in her place. May is not sure how long they sat there gazing at each other, but it felt like hours before he spoke again.

"It's getting late. There is nothing else to do, no point crying about it. We need to get you back home," he says, his voice gruff as he returns to his feet.

She stands up as well, then looks at the tack still attached to Red's body. It was her father's old saddle. The one his father had cherished and passed down to him. While May has never been the sentimental type, especially when it comes to anything that deals with her father, she cannot afford another saddle. May grimaces at the thought of leaving it there. His eyes travel from her tear-stained face to the saddle cinched to the dead horse.

"I'll come back for the saddle." His voice, sounding irritated, breaks her train of thought.

"Look, I'll take you home and come back," he pauses, adjusting his insensitive tone, "I promise."

Aside from giving him some directions back to her farm, they ride in silence. The only sounds that are heard are from the birds cooing and his horse as she breathes heavily through her flared nostrils. May cannot help but hold onto his waist to keep her balance, but she feels like she's bothering him. Regardless, she wants to squeeze the stranger, relish in the comfort of his warm presence and distract her thoughts from Red's stiffening corpse, but he's just that, a stranger.

He does not say a word when they arrive at May's farm, not even giving her his name. She shrugs it off. After all, it has been a long day. Her bed welcomes her tired and aching body. The fall had left her right shoulder and elbow bruised with some scrapes. The blue eyes of the man that helped her are all she can see when she closes her eyes. *Who is he? What was he doing in the area? Why was he out all alone?* Her mind races in circles before she drifts off into a deep sleep.

"Wait, wait, wait. Let me get this straight. Some random guy shows up, shoots your horse, and then delivers your saddle," Felix says. His words come between mouthfuls of pancake.

Felix is May's dearest friend. He was once a chubby-faced boy, but now he's tall and slender with broad shoulders. His face is thin and unblemished. Light freckles sit above his high cheekbones. His eyes are a deep green with brown flecks in them and his short hair is golden-blond. Felix is very popular with the ladies, not only because his attractive appearance, but also due to his charming personality. Felix and his father Royce own and run the town's tailor shop. Owning a sheep farm means that their shop is May's farm's biggest customer and ally.

Only a year older than her, Felix and May grew up together. As children, they would play with blocks and dress up in fabric remnants while their fathers chatted about business and personal matters. He has been there for her as long as she can remember. Felix is like a brother to her, the sibling she never had but always needed. As early as the age of nine, she would sneak out of her house and ride Red to Felix's house. They would sit in the middle of the town's square, alone but unafraid, staring at the stars and dreaming of ways to escape this small town and take on the world. He was May's rock when her father died. He never minded holding her while tears streamed down her freckled face when the stresses of the world seemed to pile on her shoulders. Felix even helped her with the flock as she learned to take care of them and the farm chores by herself.

"Can you be a little more sensitive? I just lost Red…"

He stops chewing and looks down at the table. "I'm sorry."

It has been several days since Red passed on and May encountered the quiet stranger. As promised, the man had left her saddle and tack sitting on her front porch. He had even left a lock of Red's tail, braided and tied off with a ribbon, lying on the saddle for her. May has not seen or heard about the stranger during this time. Of course she had to tell Felix about the whole ordeal, to see if perhaps he knows something about the man. However, like usual, he's just as clueless as she is.

"I mean, I didn't even catch his name," May says.

She sighs, rubbing her hands against her face.

"Why do you care about this guy so much anyway?" he asks. He seems a little envious. Before May can answer he adds, "Do you have a crush on him?"

She rolls her eyes.

"I just wanted to thank him, he went out of his way to be kind to me," she says.

May rises from her chair, taking the dirty dishes from the table and bringing them to the sink. *He was attractive.* His dark curly hair, bright blue eyes, and the dimples on his cheeks and chin are enough to melt an icicle. Not to mention he's tall, well over six feet tall. She hears a crash, muddying the man's image in her mind.

"Shit," Felix mutters.

He walks over to the sink. May feels the heat rush up to her cheeks, realizing she has dropped one of the dishes.

"I'm sorry," she says.

Her face is now a bright red as she reaches down trying to gather the broken pieces.

"It's fine, you klutz," he says.

Felix gently pushes her away from the sink, and begins picking up the mess. May puts her hand on her forehead and walks back towards the table.

"I just don't understand how a stranger comes to our small town and nobody else sees him except for me," she says.

May sits down and sighs heavily. Her fingers trace the smooth grooves on the dining table, slightly distracting her from her embarrassment.

Felix's kitchen area is quaint and inviting. The table she sits at is made from pine trees most likely cut on the outskirts of town. It's stationed in the corner of the room away from the stove and other utilities. The pots and pans are hanging neatly on the rose-colored wall, while dishes, silverware, and glasses are hidden inside the cupboards. The pine table itself is thinly coated with soft white paint. The tile flooring is white with soft pink hues, bringing the furniture and walls together. It's similar to the interior of a child's doll house. Everything has a place and nothing is out of place. Even the dishes, as he washes them, are neatly placed in a pile awaiting to be dried.

A knock is heard at the door, immediately followed by a woman letting herself in. The woman, Annabelle, is elderly and frail in appearance, but kind in the face. Her eyes are a pale, glassy blue that reflect sadness since the passing of her late husband. She never discusses her age, but she appears to be in her late sixties. Annabelle and her only son, Brian, own and run the butcher shop. In her earlier years, Annabelle was not only the face of the shop but the reason people went. She would talk customer's ears off, give discounts, and share cooking recipes. Annabelle was even the one who talked the Mayor into holding several of the town's annual festivals, such as the flower festival in the fall and the ball that takes place during the spring.

Her son is an awkward individual to say the least. Brian keeps to himself, he rarely looks people in the eyes when he does speak, and he usually can be found talking to himself. He's very tall, with a pot belly. His left eye is lazy and never looks in the same direction as his right. The poor man is probably lonely, the only company he keeps is his mother and the animals he butchers. He has never been married and has no children of his own.

"Hello dears, I hope I am not intruding. I just was hoping to introduce you to our newest partner," Annabelle says.

She gestures to the door, which opens wider as a man enters. The same man, black curly hair and all, who had helped May with Red. He's wearing a worn-out pair of pants, faded and featuring many patched-up holes, and a long-sleeve button up shirt. It's unbuttoned enough to where she can see his hairless chest, but not enough to show his muscular disposition. May bites her lip, taken aback as she immediately recognizes him.

"This is Clint. He's the new cattle farmer that just moved in to the vacant farm the Anders used to own," Annabelle says.

Clint nods and extends his hand to Felix who had approached him and Annabelle upon their arrival. Reluctantly, Felix takes his hand and shakes it. It's apparent, for some unknown reason, that her best friend does not like the cattle farmer.

"I'm Felix, and this is May," Felix says.

He signals to himself and then to May with his hands. Clint nods, his eyes are fixated on May. His stare knocks the breath out of her body, making her struggle to rise from the kitchen chair. Awkwardly she approaches him, her feet are heavy, making the short walk exhausting. Clint extends his hand to her, when their skin meets static shocks her fingertips, making her recoil slightly. A smirk forms on his face, painting her cheeks red.

"It's nice to meet you," he says.

May nods her head, nervously rubbing her upper arm.

"As much as I would like to stay and catch up with you two, we need to get back to the shop. Have a nice day, sweeties," Annabelle says.

She quickly ushers Clint out of the door. May walks over to the window, watching them as they walk towards the bank. Annabelle seems to be talking, her hands moving as she walks as if she's describing something in great detail. Clint is just walking beside her, occasionally nodding and looking towards the places she gestures to. However, he does not appear to say a word in response.

"So that's the guy?" Felix asks.

He seems to be studying May as she watches Clint and Annabelle from the window.

"Why did he not say that you two had already met? Do you think he was embarrassed or something?" Felix asks.

May turns, facing her friend, glaring.

"Maybe he didn't want to get into a long story? I'm sure he and Annabelle have more places to visit, more people to meet. Besides, we didn't formally introduce ourselves then. Why were you rude? You acted like shaking his hand was going to turn you to stone or something," she says.

His face flushes a deep red. He averts his eyes.

"I have no idea what you're talking about," he says.

May rolls her eyes.

"I know you better than that," she says.

She shakes her head at him before retreating outside and into the morning sun. A yellow butterfly with black points flutters in front of her face, quickly flying away before she can even attempt to trap it with her hands. It's a quiet day. Being that it's spring most of the town's occupants are either busying themselves with their farms and businesses, or attending the small school. The sun is shining, but a cool breeze overtakes any warmth it's providing. May shivers and huddles against her thick lambskin coat.

If only Red was here. May sighs, not looking forward to the long, cold walk back to her farm. The dirt path is well kept, even with the traffic of horses and carts that often pass through. Sometimes when it rains, carts will get stuck and leave ruts as they travel through. Usually someone rakes and works the dirt to fill in the ruts and blemishes. The dirt path mixed with rocks and small pebbles, eventually merging with stone as it gets closer to the town's square.

"Do you need a ride?" a familiar, deep voice asks.

May turns, her mouth gaping as she sees it's Clint. He sits atop his beautiful grey mare, basking in the glow of the sun. May casts her eyes to the ground, attempting to escape his piercing gaze.

"I figured Annabelle would still be busy showing you around. Did you get to see every nook and cranny of the town?" she asks.

The three main stores besides Felix's are the general store, farming and gardening store, and butcher shop. While Clint had probably had already been taken to and familiarized with the butcher shop prior to forming the partnership, Annabelle may have shown him the smaller vicinities: the school, bank, church, and bed-and-breakfast.

"Yes, she did. Your boyfriend's shop was the last on the list actually," he says.

"Boyfriend? What? Felix is my friend, we have known each other since childhood," she says.

"So do you want a ride or not?" he asks.

May nods. She walks up to Clint and his horse, once again accepting his hand. His biceps bulge as he pulls her up onto the mare. May hesitates to put her arms around him. She doesn't want to bother him, she's just a stranger after all. The pancakes in her stomach churn. *Why do I feel like this? I don't even know the first thing about him, only his name. Not to mention, if Annabelle had not shown up, I wouldn't have even had known that much.* After a few seconds, which felt more like agonizing hours, she caves and puts her arms around him.

"All right," Clint says.

He clucks at his mare, who swishes her tail before starting a brisk walk. Feeling slightly uncomfortable, May glances back behind her. She sees Felix watching her and Clint as they ride away towards the rural part of town.

"So tell me about yourself," Clint says.

May pauses, thinking before she answers. She's not sure if he wants to know about her personally or what she does in Pine Valley.

"I have lived in Pine Valley all my life. I took over my father's sheep farm after his death," she says.

"I'm sorry for your loss," he interjects.

May shakes her head, not wanting sympathy, but he cannot see.

"It has been four long years. Don't worry about it," she says. Her response is cold, not towards Clint for his response but because of her still-present feelings towards her father.

"What did you do for a living before you moved to Pine Valley?" she asks.

"I worked on a horse ranch for eleven years. Moon here is one of the last horses I broke there. I fell in love with her and had to bring her with me. She's a nice little mare, pretty good with cattle too," Clint says.

"I don't know you very well, but even a blind man could see that you are good with horses. If you worked at a ranch for eleven years, how old are you?"

"Believe it or not I'm twenty-eight."

"I can see that, not saying you look old or anything. I'm twenty-two myself. Did your parents own the ranch you worked at?"

"No... to be honest, I never met my parents. I lived at an overcrowded orphanage until I ran away to work at the ranch. I'd still take horse shit over people's lies any day."

The pair engage in small talk until they ride into the entrance of May's farm. He whoas his horse, keeping her still as May slides off the side.

"Thank you for the ride," she says.

"It's not a problem. I'll probably see you again soon... hopefully," Clint says.

He winks and flashes her a smile. May's heart rate increases. She watches him as he rides off. He seems a little rough around the edges, but like a hen's egg, he probably just has a hard shell.

Spring is arguably the busiest time of the year for a farmer. Fields need to be plowed, crops planted, and livestock with their newborns needed tending to. May has her hands full to say the least. Her twenty-five-acre farm is home to twenty-eight ewes, a ram, a donkey, two herding dogs, a coop full of hens, and a few feral cats. The acreage is fenced off into several sections. Two pastures, about ten acres each are grazed by the sheep, where the animals are free to move in and out of each section. Her house, small and modest, sits at the front of the property. It's a two-story house, holding a bedroom upstairs, a living room, kitchen, and another room in the back. The room in the back is too small to be a bedroom, it's more like a walk-in closet, but it's where May was forced to sleep as a child. Now she uses it to store extra blankets, and an old armchair.

The barn sits about twenty feet from her home. The barn has three stalls and a small wooden stock. May rotates the sheep from the pasture into the stall and then to the stock when it's time to shear them. A pile of straw sits in the corner of the barn, the wall next to it holds her shearing scissors, a rake, and sacks that hold the wool during collection and transport. An old, rusted wheelbarrow rests next to the straw. Red's tack, the saddle and blanket along with the smooth leather headstall and matching breast collar, sit on a makeshift saddle rack in the corner opposite to the wheelbarrow. The smooth snaffle bit still attached to the headstall has a piece of dried grass stuck to it. May cannot bring herself to clean it off.

This morning it's unusually warm for early March, the temperature levelling out at about seventy-two degrees. May finishes collecting the eggs from her coop and finds herself with a little bit of free time on her hands. She and Felix are going to meet up later in the day to find a dress for the upcoming town festival. The thought of hitting town early just to wait on him seems boring. May finds herself missing Red. After all, if he was still here, she would go for a ride to pass the time and relax. She decides to go to the lake.

Pine Valley's lake is not too far from her farm, about five miles down the dirt road and maybe a quarter mile left into the forested area. It's secluded, but that only adds to the attraction. May hums to herself as she walks. A smile sits on her face. Her skin embraces the warmth of the sun. Birds are chirping their own tunes as she passes the trees where they are nested.

May turns off the road and starts the short hike to the lake. The area is thick with pine trees, large and small, that she has to weave around. There are also stumps and dead trees that litter the way. Wild animals have made homes in some of the dead foliage, withdrawing reason to clean up the area. Besides, the lake is accessible to everyone but not many people venture to it. The majority of those who have not yet visited the lake are afraid of getting into poison ivy or losing their way in the maze of pines.

May hears a splash, stopping her in her tracks as she stands within twenty-five feet of the body of water. She studies the lake, wondering if someone is already there or if an animal has gone for a swim. The violets surrounding the lake are in full bloom, coloring the greenery with bright yellow and purple hues. There is a duck squabbling at her newly hatched ducklings waddling their way through the grass bordering the water. Mockingbirds and finches are singing softly in the treetops. To the northern edge of the lake is a pile of something out of place. May squints and gasps. She puts her hand over her mouth. It's someone's clothes. Her first instinct is to turn around and leave, but her curiosity is piqued. She crouches down behind the trunk of a thick tree. The cat-tails around the lake are thick and tall, but she can see a silhouette emerge behind them. The figure is a tall man with dark hair. Dark, curly hair. Her eyes widen.

"That's... that's Clint," she whispers.

Maybe she spoke louder than she had anticipated. Maybe he felt eyes staring at his muscular back; However, for whatever reason Clint turns and looks towards May's direction. She ducks behind the tree and places her hands over her mouth, hoping to conceal her breathing. *Great, he's going to think I'm some sort of a creep.* She feels unnerved. May hears the water splash and sighs. She feels slightly relieved. Maybe he hadn't heard her after all. Suddenly, she hears rustling in the grass followed by a twig snapping. She freezes again. Nervous sweat beads on her forehead. *Please, please, please be a rabbit. Be a deer, be a skunk, be anything, just not Clint.* She tightly closes her eyes, holding her breath again as she sits in limbo. With blind courage she finally wills herself to open her eyes. Clint, wearing only his underwear and dripping with water from his swim, is crouching down in front of her.

"Good morning," he says.

Clint has a smirk on his face, seemingly amused by the entire situation. May's face is as red as a tomato as she struggles to find the right words to say. She looks at his face then is drawn to his chest. Feeling her face burning with embarrassment, she looks down. Clint outstretches his hand, gently touching her chin and bringing her gaze to his. She closes her eyes in a weak attempt to avoid eye contact.

"Did you come for a swim too?" Clint asks.

May, keeping her eyes shut, shakes her head no.

"Well, that's not fun."

May opens her eyes ever so slightly, but enough to see a wild grin suddenly appear across his face.

"I think I'm going to have to show you what you are missing," he says.

Clint grabs May around the waist and heaves her over his shoulder. His biceps bulging as he constricts his arm around her waist.

"Wha-what are you doing?" May asks.

She feels a mixture of terror and embarrassment as he holds her against his damp skin. She squirms, struggling to break free from his grasp, but it's in vain. He's too strong. To her horror, as soon as Clint is knee deep in the lake, he tosses her in like a rag doll. The water that engulfs her is warmer than expected, but still shoots a chill through her entire body. She surfaces and swings her head back, throwing her hair off her face. Clint, who had jumped in deeper while she was under the water, wades up to her.

"Why?" May asks. It's all she can say.

Clint splashes water towards her. She releases a pitiful yelp.

"I thought you could use a closer look at what I was doing. You were watching me anyway," he says.

May's face reddens again and she shakes her head in disagreement.

"No, I wasn't... not at first anyway. S-seriously, I didn't mean to. I didn't know you were even here," she says.

Attempting to distance herself from him, she swims backwards. He follows her.

"So that's the story you are sticking to?"

"It's not a story. I just had some free time, so I figured I'd come to the lake."

"To spy on me?"

"No! I didn't even know you were here!"

"Then why did I find you hiding behind a tree?"

"Well... I didn't want you to see me."

"My point is proven, thank you."

"I didn't want you to see me because I figured you would think I was a stalker or something."

"I see," Clint says.

He lets a few seconds of silence go by before putting his hands on her shoulders and dunking her in the water. He's laughing maniacally as she resurfaces. She spits water towards him. Maybe it's the way May has let her guard down, or perhaps the sun is illuminating her face just right, but Clint cannot seem to stop staring at her face.

"What? Is there something on my face?" she asks.

He swims to her and gently pushes her hair behind her ear, making her eyes widen and cheeks flush.

"Nah, you're good," Clint whispers.

He weaves his fingers in between locks of her hair, cradling the back of her head. His stare paralyzes her. It's as if time has stopped and the world around them has ceased to exist. Suddenly, he brings his lips to hers. His kiss sends a shiver down her spine, raising the hairs on her neck. He pushes his mouth hard against hers. Her hands squeeze his wet, muscular forearms. His breath is sweet like honey. He pushes his hips against hers as his hand falls to her side. His fingers toy with the bottom of her shirt. He slides his hand under the fabric, reaching for her lower back. She flinches under his touch. His hand does not waver, inching higher against her skin. She pulls away from his grip and forcefully pushes him back.

"Stop," she says.

Confusion plagues his face. Her body is quivering. Clint extends his arm, caressing her shoulder. She shies away from his touch.

"I'm sorry... I wasn't trying to push you," Clint says.

She swims away from him. "It's not you, I promise. I just... I just can't."

Before he can approach her again, May is already at the edge of the lake.

"I have to go," she says. Her voice is pained.

She emerges from the water and begins sprinting back towards the dirt road, leaving Clint to wonder what the hell went wrong.

May is still soaking wet as she enters the town square, even though she has continuously tried to wring out her shirt. Her damp clothes hug her body, clinging to her waist, breast and thighs. She smells like wet grass with a hint of mud. Her mind is heavily weighted with everything that had just happened with Clint. His soft skin, gentle hands, sweet lips are locked inside her head. She fears she might have hurt Clint's feelings. It's not like she wanted to dodge his advances, but she could not allow him to see her body. Not without a warning at least. She's so deep in her thoughts she nearly walks right into Felix.

"Whoa, you look like a drowned rat," Felix says.

His eyes are wide as he studies her disheveled appearance.

She rolls her eyes. "Yeah, sure, thanks."

"Normally, I would not let someone looking like this inside my store, but I'll make an exception since it's you," he says.

Felix cannot help but snicker as he holds the shop door open for his wet friend.

The inside of Royce and Felix's shop is glamorous to say the least. Extravagant dresses, suits, hats and ties are hanging from the display walls. The counter tops are brown and copper marble, built up on the finest wood money could buy. The walls are a pearlescent white and the floors are stained to match the wooden parts of the counters and tables. Even the back room, where the sewing necessities and fabrics are stored, is tastefully arranged. As could be expected, the clothing sold there is of high quality so the prices reflect that. May is always given discounts since she's one of their partners, but she prefers the better priced, work-efficient clothing she buys from traveling seamstresses.

"All right, don't get upset, but I went a little crazy with the design," Felix says.

He provides a towel for her and ushers her towards a red embroidered chair before walking into a closet. May sits down, rubbing her hair dry with the towel. Normally she does not accept free clothes from Felix. They are far too expensive for her to take without repayment. Not to mention she never has the need to wear such extravagant clothing. However, Felix had practically begged her to let him design her a dress for the Spring Ball. The Spring Ball is an annual event where the townspeople, all dressed to the nines, gather at the town square for dancing, fine wines, and fancy snacks.

"I hope you're ready for this," Felix says.

He emerges holding a gorgeous, floor-length crimson dress. It's strapless, fitted in the waist, with a flowy skirt and adorned with a thin layer of lace around the waistband. May is speechless.

"Try it on, *please*," he says.

"Okay," she says.

May strips off her damp clothes. Felix watches and waits, ready to aid her into the dress. He has seen her body dozens of times over the course of their friendship. Felix has seen what she had kept hidden from Clint at the lake. He has seen it so many times he does not even notice anymore. Her body is covered in scars, predominately on her back. They are shades of light purple and soft reds, all standing out against her pale skin. The scars are from lashes and cuts delivered to her by her father at a young age.

May steps into the dress and he helps her pull it up. The back of the dress has ties, similar to a corset, enabling the bodice to be adjusted for May's size. Felix walks over to her and helps her tie the bodice. She walks over to the mirror to inspect the gown. It fits her like a glove.

"Now, there is one condition that comes with this dress," he says.

May tilts her head, wondering what he's about to impose on her.

"You have to be my date to the ball," Felix says.

He smirks, probably assuming she would not turn him down.

2

Chapter 2

The day for the Spring Ball has finally arrived. It has been a couple of days since May and Clint had kissed and neither of them had seen each other since. It's a comfortably warm spring day, not humid or muggy. She spends the earlier part of the day busying herself at her farm harvesting eggs, tending to the sheep, and cleaning the place up a bit. The crimson dress, as beautiful as ever, hangs in her closet waiting on her. Normally she's a wall flower at this festival, trying to blend in and stay out of couples' ways. Sometimes, with Felix's disapproval, she even skips this festival. Tonight, will be different story. Not only is she attending the event but there is no way she can blend in while wearing the gown.

Earlier in the week she had snuck into town to find accessories. May splurged on a ruby pendant with a delicate white gold chain. She did not have enough to afford the matching earrings, but she's planning on wearing her hair down, so they would not be visible anyway. May also found someone to sell her a bright red shade of lipstick that would complement the dress perfectly. She's beautiful naturally, but she finds herself plain and wants to look perfect for the ball. Even though Felix is her date, she's really getting gussied up for Clint. She's not sure if he will be attending the event or not, but in the back of her mind she knows he's the only reason she's even going.

May sits in front of the mirror and stares at her reflection. One by one she takes the rollers out of her hair, each piece releasing a gentle curl. She uncaps the lipstick and brings it to her lips. It's smooth and soft, but not as soft as Clint's lips. She cannot help but think of him. *I wonder if he will like this shade, I hope he won't think I'm trying too hard.* May lightly pads the excess pigments off with a towel. She clasps the ruby necklace on and pulls her curls from behind her ears. May takes a deep breath, staring at her reflection. She feels like a stranger is staring back at her. She's not used to seeing herself dolled up.

May leaves her vanity and goes to her closet. The dress is beautiful and extravagant, but it comes with a price. She will be obligated to spend the night with Felix regardless of Clint's presence or not. May steps in and pulls the gown up. Her flat-heeled shoes are old and discolored, but the length of the dress hides them. May steals one last glimpse at the stranger in the mirror before walking downstairs. Outside waiting on her is a horse-drawn carriage.

The carriage is gorgeous. The exterior wood is deep mahogany. Intricate swirl designs are carved into the wood. The indentations in the designs are much lighter in color, making them pop. The horses hooked to the carriage are Friesians. Their wavy manes fall past their withers. White plumes protrude from their dark-oiled browbands. White roses are attached to their neck straps. The door of the carriage is open, revealing the plum-colored velvet interior. Felix is leaning against the carriage with his top hat in hand. His golden hair is stiff, pressed against his head.

"Wow," he whispers.

He bows like a gentleman as she approaches him. She smiles and curtsies in return. He's sporting a black coat, white undershirt, black pants and a red bow tie cut from the same fabric as May's dress. He takes her hand and helps her into the carriage. The driver signals the horses and they take off. May realizes that Felix is staring at her.

"Don't get me wrong, you always look beautiful but tonight it's like you are glowing," Felix says. She blushes and averts her eyes from his stare.

"I just hope it's not *too* much, you know?"

"Nonsense, have you forgotten we are going to a ball? You can be such a pessimist sometimes, darling."

"Darling?"

"Cannot I call you that? You are my date tonight after all."

"I suppose," May says.

I hope he doesn't get any ideas. Felix is charming and she enjoys his company, but sometimes he seems like he wants to cross the line of friendship. The thought of his unrequited affection makes her stomach churn. She does not want anything to happen that would cause a rift in their friendship. Besides, he's more like a brother to her than just a typical friend. As the carriage rolls in the direction of the village square she begins to hear the soft sound of music. It grows louder and louder as they draw near. It's to the point that May cannot hear her own thoughts by the time they finally arrive at the edge of the square. Horses and carriages, all varying in size and color, border the main path. The square itself is already packed with people. Most of the guests are from Pine Valley, but there are few mixed in from visiting towns.

Oil lamps and hanging candles are strung up in the trees. Tables, strategically edged in the corners, are adorned with white crocheted table liners. Tall candles and different foods litter the tops of the tables along with bowls of punches and alcoholic mixes. A band, brought in and paid for by the bank owner Mark, are strumming their stringed instruments and blowing their flutes to a catchy tune.

Felix gently holds May's hand as she steps down from the carriage. He locks his arm with hers as they make their way into the crowd. *I can do this. I can do this.* She feels a lump in her throat grow as they merge in with the festival goers. Everyone is dressed in beautiful gowns and nicely tailored suits. The air is powdered with cinnamon, chocolate and buttered bread. The pair migrate towards the middle area, squeezing between other couples. Felix takes her right hand with his left and he places his other hand on her waist. May clings onto him tightly as they move around with the music. The song changes, couples migrate to form two different circles. Looping arms with the people next to them, May and Felix skip around in a circle. The chorus starts, picking up the beat as the fiddle's sawing intensifies. Felix and May twirl with each other before she's passed on to another partner. After a few songs Felix pulls her away from the crowd and towards the tables.

"Hi Felix!" a shrill female voice says.

They turn to see Rebecca Miller, dressed in a pale pink dress with a fluffy tule bottom, standing behind them. Rebecca is Mark's daughter. She's a short girl with brown eyes and long brown hair. Her face is pretty, but her conceited personality makes people quickly forget about her appearance.

"Oh, hello Becca," Felix says.

He scratches the back of his neck nervously as the brunette stares him down. The whole town and most likely the other close by villages know Becca has a large crush on Felix.

"I was wondering when you would arrive. What took you so long to get here?" Becca asks.

She seems to be ignoring May's presence entirely. May pushes her curled hair behind her ear.

"Well I had to go pick up May. She's my date," Felix says.

He gestures towards May. She smiles at the petite, desperate girl.

"Oh," Becca pauses momentarily before asking, "Would you like to dance with me?"

Felix takes a small step back and throws his arm around May.

"I'm here with May, I couldn't just leave her alone," he says.

May rolls her eyes. Perhaps he only invited her so he could avoid a situation like this.

"You know what, Felix? I think you *should* dance with her. It's rude to say no to a lady," May says.

She smiles as the horror spreads across his face.

"Right, it's settled then," Becca says.

Becca grins deviously as she grabs Felix's arm. She drags him away towards the band. He glares back at May. She pours herself a cup of wine and sighs. It's nice to be alone. This is not her cup of tea and she prefers the days when she had stayed home. After sipping on her wine for a little bit she decides to go look for Clint while Felix is occupied. She does not know how long he will be trapped by Becca. May has no time to wait. At first, she searches by the edges of the square, carefully avoiding dancing couples. *I doubt he will be mixed in with the crowd.* A few songs pass. She worries Felix will find her before she can find Clint. *This is useless, I will never find him.* May sighs. She feels a light tap on her shoulder. She turns around. Her friend, Nina, stands in front of her.

"Good evening May," Nina says.

Nina is a heavier girl, but she's not ashamed by her looks or the fact sugar runs through her bloodstream. Her face is blemish free and fair but has never had much luck with men. Her satin blue dress is one size too small. The fabric bunches at the waist. Her cinnamon-colored hair is fashioned in a bun.

"Hello Nina, you look lovely. Are you here by yourself or did you bring a date?" May says.

"Thank you, you do as well. Actually, I am by myself again. Who is your date?" Nina says.

"I am here with Felix, but Becca managed to kidnap him. Honestly, I was hoping to see someone else here," she says.

"Oh? Who?" Nina asks.

May's eyes scan the crowd. Felix is wearing a frown as he twirls Becca. Her obnoxious giggles echo over the band's fiddle. Still no sight of Clint.

"Just a new friend," May says.

Nina lets out a chuckle.

"A friend? If you got that dressed up for a *friend*, I can't imagine how you would dress for a lover," she says.

May's cheeks flush. She casts her eyes to the sidewalk.

"Good evening ladies."

The hairs on the back of her neck stand up. She looks up and her painted lips form a smile. Clint is standing in front of her. His white collared shirt, unbuttoned enough to expose his chest, is tucked into a pair of black dress pants. His boots are dusted in dry mud.

"Would you like to dance?" Clint asks.

His dimples appear as he smiles. May's eyes light up as she takes his hand and nods. She looks back to Nina, who winks at her. He escorts her to a corner of the square, seeming to avoid mixing in with the rest of the people dancing. Clint puts his arms around her waist and pulls her close. May takes a deep breath. They slowly begin moving, offbeat to the band. May realizes Clint's eyes are locked on her. Her heart is beating faster and faster with each step they take. The earth could have been falling apart around them and she would not have known.

Four songs are performed by the band before Clint and May stop dancing. Her legs feel a little wobbly. Hand in hand, they sneak off towards the edge of the square.

"You know, I don't know if I was doing that right," Clint says.

He laughs. His tan face reddens.

"Honestly, you were perfect," May says.

She smiles at him and squeezes his hand. Energy runs through her fingertips. Clint's confused look at the lake flashes in her mind. Her expression grows somber. She takes a deep breath.

"I really need to talk to you, in private. It's about what happened at the lake," May whispers.

She looks down at the ground, her expression unwavering.

"Listen, you don't have to explain anything. I completely understand," Clint says.

May cannot help but feel he's just saying that to make her feel better. His calloused hand touches her chin. He raises her face so that her eyes are looking into his.

"No, Clint. I really do need to speak with you about it. Please, follow me," she says.

They walk together in silence for a couple of minutes, not stopping until the once overbearing music is barely audible. The area, wound off from the main dirt path, is heavily forested. They stop at a patch of grass that is secluded by trees. May sits down and ushers for him to sit next to her. The moon is full, providing adamant light for them to see each other. Cicadas are buzzing loudly. Frogs are faintly croaking in the distance.

"You didn't do anything wrong, l-let me assure y-you," she says.

She pulls her knees to her chest and inhales a deep breath. Clint looks at her. Tears are welling up in her eyes.

"I didn't want you to see me," May says.

She pauses as the tears start cascading down her cheeks. The droplets stain her dress.

"My mother died while she was giving birth to me. My father blamed me for her death. He only had enough room in his heart for one person, her. I think I was a constant reminder of the love he lost. He became an alcoholic. The more he drank the angrier he got. He began hitting me. The beatings escalated as I got older. He would whip me until my back bled, leaving with me scars. I have ugly scars all over me."

Clint inches closer to May. He caresses her hair. Tears are heavily streaming down her face. She still has so much anger left towards her father.

"The last time he beat me was the worst. I don't remember much of it. Felix found me lying somewhere in the acreage next to my farm. I was naked and unconscious. We have no idea how long I was out there, but the temperatures were in the low forties. If he had not found me when he did, I don't know if I would be here today," she says.

The morning after that beating, her father was found dead. He had a single gunshot wound to the head. The sheriff from the town over declared John's death as suicide. May was left to slowly rebuild her life. It took her several days to recover from her father's abuse and a few weeks to have the farm operational on her own, but with Felix's help she was able to start a new chapter in her life. May wipes the tears from her eyes, her eyelashes are heavy from the moisture. She takes a few deep breaths, slowly inhaling and exhaling, to calm herself.

"I must look like a mess," she says.

May laughs half-heartedly, lightening the mood. She regains her composure.

"No May. You look as beautiful as ever," Clint says.

He traces her painted lips with his fingers before caressing her cheek. He brings his hand to the back of her head. She leans in to him. Their foreheads touch. May puts her hand to his cheek, running her hands against the black stubble. She raises her lips to his, softly pressing them together. His hand falls to her knee, his fingertips stroking the satin as his hand moves up to her thigh. She gently falls back onto the grass. His body hovers over hers. He leans down, planting kisses on her lips and neck. His head goes lower, lingering above the neckline of her dress.

"W-wait," she says.

He pulls his head up and looks her in the eyes. She takes a deep breath. Her heart is beating rapidly.

"I... I've never done this before, I don't know what... what to do," she confesses.

His lips mold into a gentle grin. He caresses her neck.

"Don't worry, I'll take the lead," he says.

Chapter 3

May is awakened by a harsh knocking coming from the front door. It's early in the morning. Crickets are faintly chirping, and owls are cooing in the distance. The sun still has several hours left before it begins its shift. Clint is asleep in bed next to her. He's unmoved by the knocking. She wraps a thin blanket over her pale shoulders and tiptoes downstairs. Cautiously, she cracks the door open. Felix, looking somewhat disheveled, is standing on the outside.

"Do you realize how late it is?" May asks. Her voice is a barely above a whisper.

"I need to talk to you," Felix says.

He brushes inside past her, without an invitation. It has been three weeks since she has last seen him. The morning after the ball, he had traveled out of town to acquire some foreign fabrics. He has bags under his eyes and his breath is stale with whiskey. His hair is a mess and his shirt is half-way unbuttoned. Felix sits down on her tan-fabric couch, making himself at home, as he always does. May lights a candle before sitting next to him. The candle's flame flickers, poorly illuminating the room.

"What is it?" she asks.

"Why are you whispering?" Felix asks.

He runs his hands through his uncombed hair.

"I have... company," May says.

She nods her heads towards the upstairs. Felix's eyes widen, and he furrows his brow.

"Let me guess, Clint," he scoffs.

"What's wrong with that?" May asks.

"Well do you really even know this guy? I mean geez I didn't realize you were so easy with letting strangers in your bed," Felix says.

Her mouth falls open.

"I-is that what you think of me?" May asks.

"Well what am I supposed to think? You left me at the ball to go screw this guy?"

"Keep your voice down!"

"I don't care if the whole town hears me, I want an explanation!"

"Since when do I owe you an explanation?"

"You owe me *everything*!"

"I don't owe you anything!" May shouts.

She's fighting the urge to cry. Felix has always been so kind-hearted. She has never heard him speak like this to anyone before.

"What's going on down here?" Clint asks.

His steps are slow and groggy. The shouting must have awoken him. Felix angrily rises to his feet as Clint walks into the room.

"I cannot believe what I am seeing. I have been there for you for over fifteen years. And then, you do this to me," Felix shouts.

He angrily points at Clint.

"I don't understand what you are talking about," May says.

Her eyes are pleading. A few stray tears slip down her cheek.

"You need to leave," Clint says.

He walks up to Felix, squaring up with him. Clint is a few inches taller than Felix, and more muscular. Felix raises his fist as if he's going to strike him but drops them to his side. He appears slightly intimidated by Clint.

"Fine, I'll go," Felix says.

He bites his lip bitterly, rushing to the door. He pauses in the doorway, clenching the handle.

"This isn't over."

Felix slams the door so roughly that the front wall of the house shakes. May sits on the couch, unmoving. She's stunned by her friend's words. Clint sits down next to her. He puts his hands on her shoulders.

"Are you okay?" he asks.

"Yes. I just don't know who that was," May says.

She wipes the moisture from her face.

"What do you mean?" Clint asks.

"For all the years that I have been friends with Felix, I have never seen that side of him. Not once. Clint, if I am being completely honest, he scared me a little. He seemed so angry, like he could have hurt me. Or worse, he could have tried to hurt you."

"Hey, don't worry your pretty little head. I would never allow him to hurt you. Besides, I can handle myself."

"I know you are stronger than he is, but what if he brought a gun or something?"

"But he did not. He has been your friend for this long I would assume he would not do anything to hurt you."

"And if he does?"

"No ifs, ands or buts May. I won't let him."

"Thank you," May says.

I hope you are right. She embraces him. Clint's words are comforting for her to hear. Regardless, in the back of her mind she cannot help but worry. Clint blows out the candle. He kisses May on the forehead before scooping her up into his arms.

"Come on, let's go back to bed," Clint says.

He carefully carries her back up the stairs. May tosses and turns under the quilt. Softly snoring, Clint is already back asleep. *If Felix has been hiding this side of him all these years, what else could he be hiding?* Her eyes fall to the window. The curtains are drawn back, allowing the starlight to illuminate the room.

The late morning sun offers new possibilities. May needs to go into town for some errands, but she does not want to run into Felix. If he's still mad, as she expects, he might cause a scene in front of the town. That is something she does not want nor need. Her eyes search the kitchen countertop. It's naked. She checks inside her cupboards. They are bare. She sighs. *Great, I do not have a choice.* With Clint coming by almost daily she finds herself going through meats and vegetables more quickly than when she's alone, but she does not mind. His company cleans out her cabinets but the joy and warmth he brings her is enough to survive on.

The air is dry, and it's slightly humid. Honeybees are buzzing busily. They latch on and off different wildflowers. May begins the long walk to town. Her mind tries to concentrate on the chirping birds and bustling squirrels rather than encountering Felix. With any luck he will be busying himself at work. Most likely he will be in bed still. Perhaps he's lying on a couch cursing his hangover. The town itself is quiet. The majority of people are at their jobs or taking care of their farms. Felix is nowhere in sight. May lets out a sigh of relief.

"Excuse me, May," someone says. It's the voice of an older gentleman.

May stops, mid-trek to the general store. It's none other than Felix's father, Royce, who has called out to her. Royce looks like an older version of Felix. They share the same blond hair and green eyes; however, he has a curled mustache. Royce is also shorter and stouter than his son. He's always well dressed, somewhat over the top. He dresses up for all occasions such as a simple stroll through the town.

"I heard you had an early morning encounter with my son. He had way too much to drink last night, I should not have even let him leave our house. I deeply apologize for his behavior," Royce says.

He shakes his head in disappointment.

"You don't need to apologize, you know that was his choice to come and berate us," May says.

She's unimpressed. Clearly, this is his attempt to clean up his son's mess. Felix is probably too much of a coward to apologize for himself.

"I believe I spoiled him as a child. He got everything he could have ever wanted. You are the one person who has ever told him no," Royce says.

Felix is all Royce has in life. Royce's wife had left him for another man just shy of Felix's fourth birthday. With no wife and no other children Royce has poured his heart and soul into raising him. Of course, he has given Felix everything he could ever possibly want and more.

"Well Felix is, no, has been a good friend to me in the past. I just don't know where this side of him came from. I had not seen it before until last night."

"Well alcohol will do that to a man."

"Can you really blame it all on the alcohol though? I don't mean to be brash, but I think it's him expressing his feelings. He wasn't nice about it, but I bet he meant every word he said."

"You are probably right, but I am still going to talk some sense into him after he sobers up."

"Good luck, he needs some, but he's so pigheaded," May says.

Royce lets out a sigh, nods, and they part ways. Royce's words are of little comfort to May. The sins of a father may pass to the son, but not the other way around. Felix is his own person and got into this mess all by himself.

The main store, which stocks a variety from dairy products and crops to cooking utensils and farm equipment, is busier today than most days. May finds herself squeezing through a group of people just to enter the building. She feels like everyone is staring at her. She wanders around the aisles aimlessly, inspecting the store's products. The store smells heavily of cinnamon with a hint of rust. Scythes, hoes, rakes and shears sit on the back wall of the interior. Shelves in the middle of the store hold crops, grains and miscellaneous cooking ingredients. Chicken feed, corn and other livestock treats are organized against a side wall. The fourth wall has shelves where villagers bring in their own crops and products to offer for sale, a small percentage of their price going to the store itself for shelving them.

Maybe they heard about Felix unloading on me earlier today. She sighs. May just wishes everyone would just mind their own damn business. Amongst the lurkers May sees a Nina by the bread and other grains. Her navy-colored dress is stained with white powder, probably flour. Her hair is messily pulled into a ponytail. *Thank God, a friendly face.* May walks to her.

"Good morning Nina," May says.

"Why hello there!" Nina says.

She shuffles the basket she's holding to her hip, so she can offer May a side-hug.

"How are you doing today?" May asks.

"I am doing well, just trying to find some things to eat for the upcoming week." Nina pauses before asking, "The real question is are you okay?"

May sighs. She brings her hands to her face. *Everyone must know about what happened last night.* Nina rests her plump hand on May's shoulder.

"I think so. I feel like I am living a dream, a nightmare really. I have known Felix for years. He has never done anything like this before. I used to think he did not possess a mean bone in his body... I am lucky Clint was there," May says.

"I would not worry too much, I heard he was drunk. I am sure he would not have talked to you like that otherwise. Is Clint the man who talked to us at the ball?"

"Yes," she says.

May's face flushes red. She has never met anyone like him before, ever. The mere mention of his name makes her heart rate elevate.

"He's handsome. What does he do around here?"

"Clint is a cattle farmer, he has been working with Annabelle and Brian ever since he moved here."

Nina's eyes shift uncomfortably to the wooden floor. May raises an eyebrow in suspicion.

"What?" she asks.

"It's nothing, really... well, it's just... you know what happened to their last partner, Jason, right?" Nina asks.

"I do not recall. I just knew he lived next door to them on those eighteen acres," May says.

"Well, I don't mean to gossip, but it was pretty bad. You and I both know Brian is not much of a people person. Anyway, Jason and Brian got into a scuff about the beef prices. Brian wanted to start charging more per pound. Jason said that was unfair. Mind you that was during the drought and the farmer's crop output were poor that year. Jason eventually broke off the partnership and started selling his meat for less, driving business from the shop and to Jason himself. This of course angered the Greys, Brian more specifically, and things got ugly," Nina says.

"I think I remember that. Jason moved away after that for some reason?" May asks.

"No, he did not move away. Jason disappeared, vanished into thin air."

"What about his business? His livestock?"

"Brian took ownership of Jason's livestock, added him to his own herd shortly after he disappeared. As if he knew Jason was not coming back."

"Really? Are you sure that was not a coincidence?"

"To me, it's too sketchy, but I guess it could be a coincidence. Who knows, maybe the rumors are just rumors. Just keep an eye out and tell Clint to be careful," Nina pauses as she realizes other customers have been overhearing their conversation, "I have to go, don't worry too much, it just never hurts to be careful."

May stands still, a little puzzled, soaking in everything Nina has said. She has never been fond of Brian, but she likes Annabelle. *I doubt she would let her son do anything criminal.* May shakes the words from her mind. Everything Nina said is gossip and probably pure speculation. Besides, she has enough to worry about as it is, and does not need a glorified horror story to add to her list.

A few days have passed now since the ordeal with Felix. May has been avoiding him like a mouse hiding from an owl. She has even been sleeping over at Clint's house, slightly paranoid her friend would show up in the middle of the night again in another drunken rage. After another night at Clint's, May sneaks away to her farm to conduct her chores. Her chickens are clucking loudly. They puff their feathers impatiently as she opens their coop. Flies buzz around the hens, occasionally attempting to land on her as she collects the eggs. Faintly, she hears footsteps behind her.

"Can we talk please?" a voice asks.

May does not have to turn around to know who is standing behind her. It's Felix. She grits her teeth.

"It depends. If you are going to yell and curse at me, you might as well turn and go. I'm not going to sit through that again," May says.

She keeps her back to him, not wanting to face him. He steps closer to her.

"I promise I will not yell or curse at you, I was out of line the other night. May, please look at me. P-please," Felix says.

May sighs. She forces herself to turn to him. Felix is dressed in a white button-up shirt. His purple cotton pants match the bouquet of hyacinths in his hand. His brow is furrowed, and his eyes are pleading.

"First off, let me confess that I was really intoxicated. Becca approached me as soon as I got off the carriage at my house. I was already dog tired, I just wanted to unload my fabrics and go to bed when she started to berate me. She started talking about how you ditched me at the ball to go be with Clint. She would not shut up about it," Felix says.

"So?" May asks.

She rises to her feet, dusting off her pants.

"So, I started drinking. I don't remember how much I drank before I came to your house, but there are a few empty bottles lying outside the shop. The more I drank the angrier I got about the whole situation."

"Angry about me leaving the ball with Clint or that I did not get a chance to tell you?"

"Both. Mainly the fact you ditched me for Clint though. I wrote him off the first day I met him."

"Because you don't like him, I cannot be with him? Is that what you are saying?" May asks.

"Drunk me said that, sober me... no. Honestly, I want you to be happy. I just do not want him to hurt you," Felix says.

May shakes her head. *He's not being completely honest with me.* Basket of eggs in hand, she starts walking back towards her house. Felix tails behind her.

"I am really, really, really, sorry. Will you find it in your heart to forgive me?" Felix asks.

May stops on her front porch, setting the egg-basket onto the wooden border. She rubs her fingers against her perspired forehead.

"We have been friends for as long as I can remember, but I have never seen you like that. Never. Do I not know everything about you? What else are you hiding?" May asks.

Felix turns on his heels, his back to her, with his hands in his blond hair. A loud sigh escapes his lips before he turns and faces her again.

"I am not hiding anything. I just messed up, dammit. We all mess up. You are the most important person in my life, May. I cannot stand what happened, and it's killing me that we have not resolved this," Felix says.

A few tears escape his eyes, staining his shirt. May's stomach churns. Seeing Felix cry is almost as bad, if not worse, as the outburst he had the other night. Her hands tremble. She wants to throw her arms around him, but resists.

"Ugh... Okay, fine! I forgive you, but you better not do anything like that ever again. If you do, you will not get off so easily," she says.

Felix practically knocks May down as he pulls her into an embrace. His arms squeeze her as if he's trying to snap her in half. She pushes him off.

"Hey, I merely said I forgave you. I did not say I was over it, yet," she says.

Felix laughs nervously. He rubs the back of his head.

"That is fair. I promise to be on my best behavior from now on... Even around your boyfriend," he says.

That night, May finds herself alone in her house. She has grown used to Clint being with her on a nightly basis. Still, she does not mind being by herself. May spent four years alone in the house after her father's death. Being alone is something she's familiar with. The wind has picked up, blowing steady and strong. Rusted copper wind chimes outside the house are ringing constantly. It's the only noise that can be heard in the house besides the flickering of candles. May walks around her house. She blows out the candles one by one as she travels from the quaint living room to the upstairs.

The room goes dark as May blows out the last candle. She hears a strange sound, something like muffled barking. She sits down the unlit candle and walks over to the window, drawing the curtains back. The moon is in its first quarter phase. It does not provide much light. All that is visible are the blurred silhouettes of her barn and pine trees in the distance. It's impossible to pinpoint where the noise is coming from. May shrugs her shoulders, pulling the curtains together, and walks over to her bed. She covers herself with a scratchy, orange afghan blanket. It's warm. Her eyes linger to the blackened ceiling, struggling to close with the foreign noise riding the gusty, southern winds. Eventually, May falls asleep.

By morning time, the wind has downgraded to a gentle breeze, leaving the wind chimes quiet only ringing every now and again and for only a few seconds. The air is a little chilly, even with the sun peeking from behind the clouds it's only about fifty degrees Fahrenheit. May's house is poorly insulated. The cold temperature is able to creep inside. During winter and spring, it's not uncommon for May to sleep in the barn. Wrapped in a blanket and sheltered by the straw, it's warmer sleeping in a horse stall than in her own bed; however, the feral cats are always unnerved when she sleeps in there. They hiss and spit as she tosses and turns in her sleep.

May has forgotten about the strange sound of the previous night. She tends to her chores as usual, first collecting the eggs and freeing the hens and then going to check on her flock. Walking towards the back section of her property she can see the sheep grazing. Her donkey greets her at the gate into the pasture, however she's not greeted by her two herding dogs. The dogs, Great Pyrenees, have lived with the flock for almost five years. They were bought as puppies from a traveling vendor temporarily set up in the village's square. The puppies were immediately introduced to the sheep and left to grow up with the herd. This ensured that the dogs would consider the sheep as part of their pack and protect them from predators. Even though they always stayed with the sheep they are always friendly and eager to greet May at the gate leading into the pasture.

"Bo? Timber? Come 'ere boys," May says.

Nothing. No sound of scurrying through the grass, no barking, no tail wagging. She shifts her weight to her left hip. Her eyes scan the pasture. The sheep have kept the grass trimmed down, but uneaten wildflowers are towering over the greenery.

"Here boys!"

Nothing still. May decides to walk the acreage to see why they are being disobedient. *They probably chased off a rabbit or field mouse.* The donkey follows, its tail swishing away at the flies. She starts towards the flock, wanting to check on them first. If something is wrong with one of the lambs, it could give insight on how long the dogs have been gone. The sheep shy away from her as she walks up, all except one. A single sheep is lying down on its side as she walks up. A strange odor, stale and similar to that of rotting fruit, is in the air. The animal's eyes are open and glazed-over. May's mouth falls open. It's dead.

She crouches down beside the lifeless animal. Flies are hovering around, buzzing loudly. Her fingers touch the stiff carcass. It's cold. The ewe's throat has been slit. Dried blood is stuck on its wool. There is no blood surrounding the animal. *It could have been killed elsewhere and then carried here*. She pictures the animal crying out. Its eyes wide as a man slashes into its neck. Whoever did this was patient, or crazy, enough to let the animal's blood drain out before moving it. *That noise I heard last night was probably the dogs barking at whoever did this. They probably took, if not killed, the dogs to shut them up.*

"I'm sorry," she whispers.

Unsure of what to do, May decides to move the animal's corpse to the barn. Hopefully, predators would not be drawn to the unprotected sheep with the carcass moved. If too many animals show up her donkey will not be able to run them off. She holds her breath in attempt to not breathe in the decaying fumes. Awkwardly, she picks up the stiff sheep.

Why would anyone do this? Was my livestock the only ones targeted? May's thoughts race around her head like angry bees in a fallen hive. Her sheep are her livelihood. Without the flock she wouldn't have an income and she would be unable to maintain her farm. Perhaps whoever did this did not realize this. No one in Pine Valley would be cruel enough to sabotage another villager, or so she hoped. The walk to her barn feels miles long as she carries the dead creature, even though it's maybe forty feet from the pasture. Finches shriek in panic and flee their nests as May enters the wooden shelter. Gingerly, she places the carcass in an empty stall and buries it with straw.

A soft sigh escapes her lips. She feels a small bit of comfort in the fact that she does not know what happened to Bo and Timber. *Perhaps they were not killed like the ewe and instead were taken and tossed out somewhere in the country-side.* At least in that scenario they had a chance. Ignorance is bliss, it's probably best that the ugly reality of what happened to them is a mystery to her.

Chapter 4

Hours have passed since the discovery of the dead animal and May's nerves have not calmed. Her skin feels slimy. It does not matter how many times she submerges her hands in water the texture of the ewe will not leave her fingertips. Even though she knows Clint is most likely tending his cattle or busy with ranch work, she decides to go see him. Just hearing his smooth voice or catching a glimpse of him will be enough to ease her mind.

A few unfamiliar faces pass her on the dirt path. One of the strangers is a rugged old man, face worn with time, riding a bay mule. He has a stern look plastered on his face, but he smiles as he passes May. With each new face a suspect is brought into the mix. Perhaps this heinous act has been done by a visitor, someone who held nothing personal against her. The picture of her sheep with its throat slashed, empty eyes and protruding tongue, haunts her. Not even the sight of blue jays, spreading their wings and gleefully chirping at one another, can replace the image in her head. Suddenly May begins feeling sick to her stomach, her knees buckling as she attempts to balance herself against an old tree.

Her throat burns as she unsuccessfully tries to refrain from vomiting. She did not have much to purge. She has not eaten since the morning.

Can I catch a break? May wipes the sweat beads off her forehead. She's overcome with dizziness and needs to lay down. She's already close to Clint's farm so there is no reason to turn back now. Slowly she walks, concentrating on the ground in front of her, making her way to his farm. The sight of the barbwire fence surrounding his acreage is a warm welcome to her. She makes a left at the fork of the road, leading into Clint's yard.

No Clint. She sighs. Her eyes long for him. The only sign of life is a field mouse. It's scurrying through the unkempt grass towards Clint's house. His house is old, but charming. There is no front porch, only some large rocks used as stepping stones placed in front of the greying wood exterior. The roof has been patched in several places, the repairs are a shade considerably darker than the original. Four large windows sit at the front of the house, giving a nice view from the inside.

May enters the house, which is unlocked as usual, and makes her way to the back room, the master bedroom. It's a messy, disorganized room. Discarded clothes, most of which need a good wash, are scattered about the floor. Muddy boots, missing their pairs, are awkwardly thrown about. The furniture is scarce, only a bed and wooden dresser occupying the space. Tattered curtains are drawn back, allowing the early afternoon sun to break through the window and kiss the wooden floorboards.

May kicks off her shoes and climbs onto his unmade bed. Clint's blankets and pillow smell like him, his sweat and sweet breath. The scent is more enamoring to her than a bottle of wine is to an alcoholic. Within a few minutes she finds herself at peace.

May wakes up from her dreamless sleep, rubbing her hands against her eyelids. She's unsure of how long she had dozed off. The sun is now sinking into the west. Clint should be home by this time, or at least returning soon. May stretches her arms outwards as she slowly moves through the short hallway into the living room.

The room is furnished with a tan leather couch, matching loveseat, and red fabric armchair. A glass-top pine table with one leg shorter than the other three, causing it to wobble, is centered in the room. Half-empty coffee mugs, a plate holding a partially eaten sandwich, and a pair of rusted spurs sit atop the table. Clint is slumped over on the tan couch, eyes closed and his hands folded.

"Clint?" she calls out.

Clint immediately opens his eyes and smiles at her.

"Hello sleepy head. I found you about an hour ago, I hope I didn't wake you," he says. His voice is tender and affectionate.

May sits down next to him. He puts his arm around her shoulder.

"I'm sorry I just showed up out of the blue," May says.

Clint shakes his head.

"Do not be sorry. You are always welcome here," he says.

May smiles. She runs her hands through his curly hair. He leans in, softly kissing her cheek.

"Thank you, Clint, I appreciate that. I have a reason for coming today though. Something happened at the farm."

"What? Are you hurt? If Felix did something—" Clint says.

"No, no I am fine. Felix and I are back on good terms. He came and apologized, yesterday. I heard the sincerity in his voice."

Clint's eyes widen.

"That surprises me, he seems like the type to hold a grudge... Wait, then what happened?" he asks.

"He's not, I promise. Well I went out to check on the flock this morning per usual and Bo and Timber weren't there to greet me. I called and called for them, but they never showed up. Since they were not there, I decided I better check on the sheep to gauge how long they might have been missing, and that is when I found it..."

Clint straightens his back, a serious expression shaping his face.

"One of my ewes had been killed... by a person. There is no way an animal could have done that to her," May says.

"What do you mean? Done what?"

"Her throat had been slashed but there was not any blood around its corpse. I image whoever did it, waited for the blood to drain before bringing her back to the main pasture," she says.

"Are you serious? Do you think the dogs would have torn into the person?" he asks.

"Maybe, you know they are aggressive when protecting the sheep. But the person could have disposed of them before hurting the ewe. I thought I heard something last night, but I could not see anything from my window, so I went back to bed. I really hope they are okay."

"I do too, but May you cannot blame yourself for that. In a place like Pine Valley the worst thing you can encounter is a bear. Even then you are more likely to run into a skunk rather than a bear. What did you do with the ewe's body?" he asks.

"I put it in a stall in my barn. I wanted you to see it before I did anything with it."

"Good, you know with my familiarity with the butcher shop I will be able to judge how experienced the person is. Why don't we eat dinner and then head back to your place? If you want, I'll stay the night to help keep an eye on things."

"Thank you. I do not have much of an appetite, but I probably should try and eat something," May confesses.

Clint leads her into the kitchen, ushering her to the dining table. He had cooked the food earlier. While Clint fills the glasses with water, May finds herself staring at the table prepared before her. The plates and silverware are all mixed, not a single dish from the same collection. The only thing tying them together is the fact they are all evidently used and quite old. They most likely belonged to whomever owned the property before Clint. Regardless of the tableware, the food is no less palatable. It's a stew composed of beef, carrots, potatoes, beans and rice. The carrots' fumes are powerful, but do not overwhelm the beefy odor. It's savory, but the image of the dead ewe prevents May from eating even a fourth of the bowl. She takes care of the dishes while Clint goes out and saddles Moon.

"Are you ready to go?" Clint asks.

May smiles and nods. She trots over to Clint, already on horseback. He pulls her up onto the horse. She wraps her arms around his waist and nestles her face into his back as the horse begins walking. Riding double with him has become one of May's favorite things to do. She always feels safe when Clint is near. There is just something about him that she has never experienced before and like a moth to a flame, she's drawn to him. They ride in silence to her farm, but it's not awkward like the first time they met. Instead, it's peaceful.

The moon has risen by the time they make it back to her farm. It's providing some light, but not enough to see farther then fifteen feet in front of them. As they make it into the barn the only noises to be heard are their breaths and the buzzing sound of flies. There is a peculiar stench radiating from the sheep's carcass. May lights a lantern and brings Clint into the stall. He gets down on his knees, swatting away at the flies, and begins examining the ewe. Clint traces the cut with his calloused fingers, it's clear and precise. Maggots have made the dead beast their home, shamelessly feeding on it. May gags. She averts her eyes as Clint finishes looking the animal over.

"All right May, I have seen all that I need to. Why don't we go inside? I can get rid of the carcass tomorrow morning," he says.

"All right, but first let me put Moon in this vacant stall. I don't think it's safe to turn her out giving the circumstances," May says.

She leads the grey mare into the third stall, the farthest from the dead ewe. She tosses over some hay to the horse who quickly begins nibbling at the green and yellow stalk. Arm around her thin shoulder, Clint escorts May back to her house. The pair go to the living room. Clint sinks into the fabric couch.

"Honestly May, whoever did this, knew what they were doing. Shoot, I would even reckon they are a butcher by the cut they made," he says.

May sets a lit candle onto the dark-stained end table. She falls into the cushion next to him.

"Are you certain they are a butcher?" she asks.

She knows good and well the only butcher in Pine Valley is Brian; however, considering Brian is partnered with Clint it would be surprising if he's the culprit. An image of Nina flashes in her eyes. *What about Jason?* Her stomach gurgles.

Clint shakes his head.

"I feel like I don't even have to say what you are thinking, I know. This whole scenario is just plain weird. Honestly, I would suggest Felix. I know you said he apologized, but..."

May shakes her head sternly, stopping him before he could finish his statement.

"I would bet my flock that he had nothing to do with this. Not only would it hurt his business but also there is no way he would have the stomach to do this," she says.

Seemingly assured by her words, he leans back on the couch's stuffed back.

"That means there are only two possibilities then. The butcher from Pine Valley did it, or a butcher from another town. I get that Brian is not, what can I say, uh... normal, but why would he want to kill a sheep from my girlfriend's flock?" Clint asks.

May's face flushes, heat rushing to her cheeks, catching his attention.

"What?" he asks.

"Nothing, it's just you called me your girlfriend," she says.

Confusion plagues his face. His eyebrows draw together underneath his curly bangs.

"Well... I... I mean you are. Aren't you?" he asks. His tone hits a higher pitch, suddenly seeming unsure of himself.

May laughs and thumps him on his tense arm.

"Of course," she says.

A sigh slips past Clint's lips, his form relaxing. May leans in and kisses him delicately.

"Listen, I don't want to jump to any conclusions. Especially any that would jeopardize your work. For now, just keep an eye out and see if Brian is acting any differently," May says before adding, "and please be careful."

"Hey, don't worry about me. I can take care of myself and you," he says.

May smiles and squeezes his hand.

"I know you can," she says.

They rise from the couch and Clint follows May upstairs. She feels weak, the stress from the day has taken a toll on her.

Her bed welcomes her. The night itself is quiet, unlike the previous night. No abnormal noises, only a cricket chirping a lullaby. May is tired, but she struggles to fall asleep. Her head is nestled against the feather pillow, Clint's arm is underneath her neck. Warmth is radiating from his naked body, trapped under the sheets. He stirs. The heat rises as his hand caresses May's forehead.

"I think... no, I most certainly am, falling in love with you May Ferrothorn," Clint whispers.

His lips brush against her hair and linger. Eyes still shut, May smiles and squeezes his hand. She does not have to say anything, Clint must know she's in love with him too from the way she looks at him. It does not matter May had lived twenty-two years without a single boy crush. She knows in her heart that this is what love is. A feeling she has never felt for another human before. It's a feeling that she hopes will last forever.

May finds herself standing alone in a field. It's vast and empty, the only thing visible to her is trees. She takes a few steps forward, suddenly hearing a popping noise. She spins around. Black smoke is emerging from behind the trees. Curiosity calls her. She begins to walk towards the smog. A strange stench is coming from the same direction. May quickens her pace. An uneasy feeling is blossoming in her stomach. As she draws near, she sees the carcasses of sheep littering the field. From a distance it looks they were shot, and then scorched. The flames that once encompassed them have died out, leaving it up to the buzzards to finish them off. Her attention is brought to a tree about twenty feet in front of her. There is something hanging from a branch, burning. *What is that?* May sprints forward. Her blood runs cold. It's a human body. It's not just any human body, it's Clint. The air is sucked out of her lungs. He has been strung up. A noose is tightly constricted around his neck. Before she can reach the tree to free him his body is engulfed entirely in the flames.

May screams, jolting up in her bed and from the false reality out of her dream. Her body is covered in a cold sweat as she sits there trying to catch her breath. The morning sun is pushing through the curtains, tinting the floor a yellow-orange color. She reaches for Clint, who had been asleep next to her, but he's gone. There is an indention in the mattress where his body had been, close to hers, but that is the only trace of him.

"Clint? Where are you?" she calls out, her voice panic stricken.

No answer. She rushes downstairs, taking on two steps at a time, her heart beating at least a hundred beats per second. The smell of scrambled eggs and bacon grease fill her nostrils as she hits the bottom of the stairs.

"Clint?"

Turning the corner, she finds him. He's standing shirtless in the kitchen, fixing breakfast. Seemingly oblivious of her night terror, or even her presence for that matter, he continues cooking. May rushes upon him and wraps her arms around his waist, causing him to flinch.

"Geez, you scared me," he says.

May stands there, heart rate slowly stabilizing, with her face buried in his back. He shuffles the eggs, bacon and sausages onto two plates. Her grip refuses to weaken.

"What's wrong?" Clint asks.

He turns and sees her distraught face. Her eyes are heavy with moisture, struggling to hold in tears.

"I... I had a nightmare. You were..." May says. She shakes her head, not wanting to complete the statement.

"I was what?" he asks.

She adverts her eyes from his and whispers, "You were dead."

Clint wraps his arms around her, affectionately stroking her lower back.

"And when I woke up you were gone... and when you didn't answer me, I just knew," her voice breaks off as gentle tears begin sliding down her cheeks.

"May, please look at me. I'm not dead, it was just a dream. I'm all right, I promise," Clint says.

His arms are still holding her tightly. May looks at his face, causing her tears to grow from drops to a steady stream.

Clint cups her face in his hands.

"It was a dream. I promise, no I swear on my life, I'm not going anywhere."

She wipes her eyes, red and puffy from crying, and forces a smile to her thin lips.

"I'm sorry, I know I am terribly high maintenance," May says.

"Nah, you're perfect," he says.

Clint flashes a cheesy grin which makes her giggle as her cheeks redden.

"Why don't you sit down, the food is ready. Afterwards I will find a spot to bury the ewe," he says.

May shakes finger at him.

"I will eat, but you are not going to go bury her by yourself. I am coming with you," she says.

"Works for me," Clint says.

May wraps the sheep in old linens and binds them to it with old ropes. She hopes that with the fabric, in addition to being buried somewhat deep, predators would not attempt to dig the animal up. They decide to bury the carcass on the uninhabited acreage next to May's property in case wild animals smelled it and decided to come looking. The land is covered in wild flowers, pastel pink buttercups and orange Indian paintbrushes. It's quiet, their breaths and the buzzing of small bees is all that can be heard. Clint started digging with the shovel while May sits with her knees pulled to her chest. She would have eagerly assisted him with the burying process, but there is only one shovel between the two of them. At least she's there to keep him company.

"All right, I think this is deep enough," Clint says.

May rises and inspects the hole. It's at least five feet deep and three feet wide. An earthy smell is floating above the moist dirt. She grabs one end of the bundled body, Clint grabbing the other. They gently lower it into the hole. Together they cover it. May kicks the dirt back into the crevasse while Clint continues to use the shovel. They pause, both staring at the dirt covering the ewe, giving it one last glance, before beginning the walk back to May's farm.

May is quiet and withdrawn, still shaken by the dream she had earlier. Her body is tense, flinching as Clint reaches out and touches her shoulder.

"Are you all right? You have not been yourself today," Clint says. Worry is evident in his tone.

May sighs, shaking her head.

"It's not like there is anything physically wrong. I just am feeling stressed," she says.

"This was probably an isolated incident, maybe even a cruel prank. I don't think you should worry, but you should definitely stay on your toes. Watch for anything or anyone being suspicious. I will be too, and I promise I will not let anything happen to you. Period," he says.

His words are met with silence, prompting Clint to drop the shovel and embrace May, whom in return grips tightly onto him.

I pray that you are right. She closes her eyes and relaxes into his arms.

5

Chapter 5

The spring days have melted into summer nights. It has been two months since May's sheep was killed and her dogs' disappearance. In this time there have been no further incidents, prompting Clint and May to think it was done by an individual not native to Pine Valley.

"Do you *really* have to leave?" May asks.

The morning sun is peering in through the window. It's a little after seven. May and Clint have just finished eating breakfast. May's plate of eggs and sausage looks almost untouched. Her appetite evading her.

"Unfortunately, I do. It's... for the benefit of my farm and business. Besides darling, it will only be a week, maybe two weeks tops," Clint says.

He reaches across the table and grabs her hand, squeezing it. May sighs. She abandons the table and walks into the living room. Clint follows her. He places his hands around her from behind.

"Ever since you came to town, I have gone maybe two days without seeing you. I don't mean to be childish, I just cannot image going a day without you. How will I survive two weeks?" she asks.

She puts her arms over his, pressing them tightly them against her.

"This will not be easy for me either. I love you so much May. I knew there was something special about you the moment I laid eyes on you, but I did not realize how much you would change my life. You are like a flame and I am nothing more than mere wax, melting in the presence of you."

"Clint... I love you too," May whispers.

She turns to face him. He's withholding tears in his eyes. She kisses him softly on the lips and then embraces him as tightly as she can. A couple of tears escape from his eyes as he leans over and kisses the top of her head.

"When are you leaving?" May asks.

She's still holding him, but no longer wishing to protest his absence.

Clint sighs before answering, "As soon as I go and saddle Moon I will be heading out. I have a long ride ahead of me."

May fights the urge to sigh, even though she's disappointed with his answer.

"I wish you told me last night..."

Clint squeezes his arms around her.

"I know, but I did not want to ruin the evening," he says.

"... I understand. What about your farm? Do you need me to take care of anything?" she asks.

Clint shakes his head.

"Brian is going to be keeping an eye on things for me."

He probably would have asked May, but did not want to burden her. May follows Clint outside. The grass is wet with dew. A few crickets chirp faintly. She watches him with Moon. He's tender with the horse, brushing away the dirt and dust on her dappled coat before saddling her. Clint leads the horse out, her tail swishing at a mosquito. May trails behind. Her movements are stiff and reluctant. He turns and faces her. His hand cradles her chin, pulling her to look him in the eyes.

"I promise, I will be back soon," he says.

May pulls him into a tight embrace. He kisses her before pulling away. She watches him ride off, remaining frozen in place until she can no longer see him. May's heart feels tight and pained. After standing there for what seemed like hours, May forces herself to start on her chores. She does not consider the chickens or the sheep good company, but by tending to them she at least is able to keep her mind busy.

After her chores she decides to go into town and see Felix. They are on better terms now, but it had been a couple of days since they last spoke. Being this time of day, early afternoon, she knew he would be in the tailor shop. The sun is shining bright, showing no mercy with its unrelenting heat. By the time May makes it into town she's wet with perspiration. Days like this make her reflect on the necessity of having a horse. She rolls up her sleeves of her blouse, a lightweight pale blue button up, and enters the store. As expected, Felix sits behind the granite counter. He's leaned over yellowed parchment, his face pulled in a concentrated expression, drawing. May's presence pulls his attention from his work. His lips curl into a coy smile.

"Hey, what are you doing here?" Felix asks.

"I had some time on my hands and I figured since it has been a while, I would grace you with my presence," she says.

Felix chuckles. He slaps his knee, hidden under his tan cotton britches. His shirt's sleeves, a stiff white with gold accents, are smudged grey with charcoal.

"Please have a seat," he says.

Felix ushers her to a fancy embroidered sofa that sits near the hanging garments on display. May sits down while Felix puts away an unorganized stack of designs that had been on the counter. The shop is immaculate. Soft white carpet is spread on the floor, a neutral tone to not distract customers from the colorful fashions hanging on the walls. There are mirrors everywhere. Several sketches, by Felix, are framed above the garments.

"What have you been up to?" May asks.

Felix pushes his tousled hair back. His fingers, also covered in charcoal, leave faint prints on his forehead.

"Just working, nothing exciting. Becca keeps coming over to annoy me. It's gotten to the point where I hide under the counter while my father shoos her out. What about you?"

"Sounds like my days, minus Becca coming to my doorstep. Maybe one of these years she will take a hint, or perhaps you will eventually cave in to her."

"No, never could I be that desperate. How is Clint? I do not see him around much," Felix says.

"Clint is well, he has been particularly busy here lately though. He went out of town this morning. Some business-related trip I think," she says.

"Oh. That is why you came, you are lonely."

May rolls her eyes.

"Come on Felix, it's not like that."

"Relax, I am kidding. How long will he be gone?" he asks.

"A week, maybe two weeks at the most. It will be the longest we have been apart since he came to town," she says.

"How will you ever survive?"

Dramatically, he throws his arms in the air.

"Don't make me roll my eyes, you know good and well that I will be just fine."

"I am sure you will be. Regardless you know that if you need anything I will be here. It does not matter if he's out of town or not, I am always here for you."

"I know, and I appreciate that," May says.

She truthfully does cherish his friendship. Even with his high-maintenance and sometimes entitled behavior he's her best friend and someone she knows she can count on. Before they can say anything else, the bell on the front door chimes as none other than Becca herself walks in.

"Shit," Felix mutters.

Clumsily he attempts to hide himself beside the couch. May covers her mouth in attempt to muffle her laughter. The petite girl approaches the counter. Becca's brown hair is slick against her head, fashioned in a tight braid. She's wearing a white cotton dress and lace-up boots that have never seen mud in their lives.

"What are you doing here?" Becca asks.

An ugly scowl plasters across her face. Before May can reply, Royce comes up from the back. A strip of pearly white fabric is draped over his neck.

"Ma'am I have to ask that you please stop coming in unless you are wanting to do business with us. This is the fourth day straight you have come in to harass my son. You may come inside if you wish to purchase something, if not consider yourself uninvited. I don't have time to deal with this," Royce says.

Becca's scowl transforms into a pout. Her eyes scan the room, stopping at Felix's head, which is peeping out from behind the couch. His eyes look away from hers. She scoffs.

"Fine," she says.

Dejectedly she obeys, but she slams the door so roughly that a few gowns fall from their hangers.

"Thanks Dad," Felix says.

He stands up and brushes himself off.

"No problem son. And how are you doing Miss May? Did I hear that your boyfriend is out of town?" Royce asks.

He bends down to pick up the fallen dresses, a crack erupting from his bones as he does. The interior of the store is not warm but sweat stains are present under his armpits and above his fleshy stomach.

"I am doing well, thank you. And yes, he is, but not for too long," she says.

Her eyes follow him as hangs the clothes back up.

"That is good, you just be careful. I still do not know how a pretty thing like you manages to hold up all by yourself," Royce says.

Felix interjects before May can speak, "Seriously Dad?"

"I did not mean any harm. You know we are both here for you if you ever need anything," he says.

Royce fidgets with his golden mustache, seemingly lost in thought, before retreating into his workspace.

"I am sorry, you know he's... protective," Felix says.

He sighs as he sits back down by his friend.

"I am not sure if that is the word I would have used," she says.

Looking down at her hands, May uncomfortably fidgets with her thin fingers.

"I know but I am sure we can make it up to you, with dinner or something. How does that sound?" he asks.

"That is thoughtful of you, but I do not want to be out late by myself. I should probably be on my way now anyway," May says.

May rises and migrates to the door. Felix follows her. He puts his hand softly on her shoulder.

"All right, but please do not hesitate to come here if you need anything," he says.

A couple of days have passed with May spending most of her time alone at her farm. The only time she leaves is to visit the lake. She does not mind being alone, but is missing Clint with every fiber in her body. Each day that passes leaves her feeling depressed and withdrawn. On the fourth day of his absence May wakes up a little later than normal.

"Shoot," she mutters.

The sun has already been out for a few hours. During summer months the earlier it's in the morning, the easier it's to do her chores. By nine o'clock the temperatures are already rising. Just walking to the coop and back will produce a light sweat. May strips off her gown and pulls up her pants. Hastily, she slips into a shirt and laces her boots. Deciding to skip breakfast to make a start on her chores, she rushes to the front door. As she creaks it open, she screams, horrified by what she sees.

There are chickens everywhere. Dead poultry are littered across her front porch and yard. Gizzards, hearts, livers and other innards of the birds have been removed and strung out by their corpses. Flies buzz over and around the lifeless poultry, enticed by the putrid smell coming from them. Blood is everywhere. On the grass, the birds, her porch and even the exterior walls of her home. A small carving knife, covered in dried blood, is stabbed into the doorframe. Probably the knife that had been used to kill all the birds. The smell is worse than the sight. Decay and blood are potent and mask the muggy air.

"Why?" she asks. She cannot say anything else.

Confusion plagues her. She's completely caught off-guard by the cruel and senseless act. The hens provided eggs, for which May keeps and uses as food source. By owning the chickens, she's spared from having to buy or barter eggs from another farmer.

May unfreezes herself and hurries to the coop, to see if the savage has left any survivors. Unfortunately, the assailant did not even leave her the eggs. The eggs she would have collected for the day are splattered and smashed all over the interior of the henhouse. The smell of stale yolk and blood protrudes from the inside. Her stomach churns. A feeling of uneasiness washes over her. *What if they are still here?* She shudders. *I have to get out of here.* She rises to her feet, cautiously moving away from the coop. Her mind reels with thoughts, trying to hurriedly decide where to go. Felix's face flashes in her mind, his voice echoing the words, "Do not hesitate to come here if you need anything."

May begins sprinting in the direction of the village's square. Her footsteps and the fading chirps of mockingbirds pierce the silence.

By the time the tailor shop is in sight, May's clothes are damp with sweat and she herself is out of breath. As she's opening the door, Felix is right on the other side about to exit. Startled by her sudden appearance, he jumps.

"Geez did you have to sneak up on me?" Felix asks.

His face flushes and his expression of shock shifts to embarrassment.

"I need your help," May says.

She tries to grasp her breath. Felix looks her up and down, taking in her sweaty body and distraught expression. He leads her to the bench positioned outside the shop and sits her down.

"What happened?"

"I don't know. I woke up this morning, late. And when I stepped outside, my yard had become a chicken graveyard. Every chicken in my coop is slain and littered about my property."

Shock once again engulfs his face.

"You are kidding, please tell me you are kidding right now. Why would someone do this? And who in their right minds would have done that?" he asks.

"I wish it was not true, but I can show you. I was not sure if they were still lurking around my farm so I came here as quickly as I could. I am a little afraid to go back. And honestly, I do not know how this happened, but I believe this is the same person from before," she says.

"Before? You mean this is not the first time?" he asks.

"Oh... that is right. I forgot to tell you. Are you free?"

"For you, any time. Why?"

"Walk with me back to my farm and I will tell you everything. It's a very long story," May says.

Felix nods and stands up, lightly putting his arm around May's shoulder. As they walk May tells him about the strange noises during the night followed by her dogs' disappearances and the dead ewe. She explains how Clint helped her keep an eye on things for a while but after a month of no further incidents they assumed she was safe and whomever killed the sheep had left. Felix listens, for once in his life he's speechless as he processes her words. By the time they arrive back at her farm, he's all caught up.

"I really wish you would have told me sooner. I could have helped too," Felix says. Jealousy frames his words.

"Honestly, after this, I wish I had too," she says.

May and Felix begin invading the grotesque site of the mutilated birds. They collect the chickens one by one, carefully placing their bloody and stiff corpses in an old wheelbarrow, so they can be moved off the property. She does not need their scent to attract coyotes or any other predators to her farm that might attack her sheep. They stuff twelve dead hens in the wheelbarrow, every single chicken she owned. They bring the birds and a shovel to the same land area where Clint and she had previously buried the ewe. The dirt mound that once signified where the sheep is buried is now overtaken with grass. Randomly, May picks a spot in the field and begins digging. The dirt is dry and packed, making it difficult to dig. *I wish Clint was here. He's better with this kind of stuff...*

"Let me help," Felix says.

May is surprised as he takes ownership of the shovel and starts where she left off. May watches as her friend breaks into the ground with ease, again surprising her. Felix realizes she's watching him with an astonished expression across her face.

"Oh, come on, you don't really think I am just a pretty boy, do you?" he asks.

He uses his sleeve to wipe the perspiration from his fair-colored forehead.

"I mean you helped me out when my father died, but other than that I have never seen you really work a day in your life," May admits.

Her eyes travel down at the ground.

"It's okay, a lot of people underestimate me," Felix says.

He releases a sigh and continues to dig. After a few minutes of shoveling dirt, taking a break and returning to shoveling more dirt they decide the hole is ready.

"Should we just dump them in? Or do you want them neatly placed?" Felix asks.

May grabs the wheelbarrow, tilting it, letting all the birds fall in. There is no more kindness to be offered for the dead creatures.

"All right then," Felix mutters.

He begins the task of covering the poultry mountain with dirt. After the hole is completely covered the two friends walk back to May's farm in silence. May pushes the wheelbarrow back into the barn while Felix heads to her house. He stops at the entrance to her house and pulls the knife out of the doorframe.

"Is this what you think was used to kill them?" Felix asks.

Cradling the weapon in his hands he follows her inside to the kitchen. Eggs, collected from the days prior, sit in a woven basket on the white counter. A mug, substituting for a vase, holds butterfly milkweed with orange blooms on the center of the kitchen table.

"Yes, it's the only weapon that I found. Besides, it's covered in blood," May says.

She offers him a glass of water. Felix thanks her but he continues to be preoccupied with the knife. Intently staring at the object, his eyes suddenly widen, and he swallows air.

"Is everything okay?" she asks.

May furrows her brow. She has known Felix long enough to know when something is amiss with him. He went from being his normal, chipper self to a quiet shell.

"It's... n-nothing. I promise, nothing," he says.

She shrugs her shoulders and sits down in one of the pine chairs.

"I really appreciate how much you have helped me today, which makes this harder for me," May pauses, looking him in the eyes, "but I have to ask. I know it will be an inconvenience for you, but is it possible that maybe you could stay with me until Clint gets back? I thought I would be okay alone, but after this I am not so sure."

Felix puts the knife on the table, seeming to forget his previous concerns.

"I would be more than happy to stay with you," he says.

He puts his hand over hers and squeezes it softly. His hands are much softer than Clint's, lacking the evidence of a hard day's work.

"Thank you, I knew I could count on you," May says.

Relief washes over her. A possible threat looms over her, but she knows she will feel safer having someone else there with her, especially since Felix is a male presence. She hopes the sick individual who killed the chickens will not return. Not wanting to be alone for even just a moment, May travels back into town with Felix as he goes to collect a few belongings for his stay. Being unsure of how long he would be staying at May's house, Felix sets aside several shirts and a couple of pairs of britches, nothing fancy due to the fact he wants to help her around the farm as much as possible.

When they were children, they spent many nights together. Back and forth between their two houses, May and Felix rotated overnight play sessions. At most they would spend four nights together, at minimum they would have a sleepover only once per week. When they stayed at May's farm, they would have to be quiet and courteous to not disturb and anger her father. They would pretend they were asleep and then sneak outside during the wee hours of the morning. Under the stars and away from the house neither of the friends had to worry about John's temper. More times than not they would even find themselves falling asleep in the pasture and being awakened by the rooster crows. Upon the morning sun's appearance and the rooster's beckoning, May and Felix would then tiptoe back into the house and into her bed where they went back to sleep until breakfast. This stay, in contrast, is far from the realms of their childhood memories. On the positive side, it will be just the two of them. On the other hand, going outside is not an option. As children the only fear they possessed was a whipping or lecture by John. Currently, the threat they face is unknown. Someone who is bold enough to kill a sheep and take her dogs and then murder her chickens and lay them at May's doorstep is far more dangerous and perhaps even more unstable compared to her abusive father.

By the time the friends arrive back at May's farm the sun is setting. The wind is dying down and the air itself is cooler. Crickets are crawling out, preparing themselves to serenade the night air.

"I presume I am taking the couch?" Felix asks.

He lays his belongings down on a rocking chair in the living room.

"That probably would be best," May says.

After dinner Felix retires to the couch and May goes to her bedroom. The images of the mutilated bodies that belonged to her dead hens keep flashing through May's mind as she tosses and turns in her bed. She's tired from the long day, but she also finds herself unsettled not being able to fathom why it happened in the first place. May begins concentrating on the darkness when she closes her eyes in attempt to clear her mind and relax. After almost an hour she finally finds herself drifting to sleep. Felix, however, sits up in the darkness.

6

Chapter 6

It was a very frigid morning, the day Felix found May naked and lifeless in the woods. After maliciously whipping his daughter with a bullwhip, John had dragged her lifeless bare body into a vacant lot thick with trees. He abandoned her as a slow drizzle began and returned to his home. Sitting in silence as he binged on stale alcohol. May was supposed to come see Felix for lunch, but he began to worry after noon passed, then twelve thirty, and finally one o'clock. It was not like her to be so late, and an uneasy feeling began stirring in his gut. Felix draped himself in a warm coat and headed over to her farm. By now she had been alone for several hours and the drizzle had gotten thick and heavy. The sky was colored in hues of grey. The soft pitter-patter of rain was the only noise to be heard, as the birds were quietly huddled in their nests. Upon arrival, he immediately approached the house. There was no answer as he tapped on the front door. He peeked in through a window.

The curtains were not drawn, but the house was dark, something unusual for this hour of the day. Felix squinted at a figure in the living room. The silhouette of the person was too massive to be his friend. *Looks like John.* Felix crossed his arms and paced the front porch, trying to think of where May might be. *Maybe she's in the barn.* He rushed over. Small chunks of flesh and blood splatter were scattered across the dirt floor. Red poked his head over one of the stall's door, and nickered at him. Out of the corner of his eye he saw the bull-whip, lying atop the straw. He ran his fingers over the whip and as he pulls away his hand was tinted red.

"Son of a bitch," Felix said.

Anger overcame him. He knew all too well what had oc-curred. He clasped the whip and turned to go inside and beat John with it, but stopped in his footsteps. Muddy boot-prints were leading past the barn and back to the house. *Where did you go?* He looked back towards the house. *Dammit, John must have taken you somewhere else.* He assumed he could find his friend at wherever they originated from, and began walk-ing the path left by the prints.

The brush got denser the farther the trail led away from the farm. Felix had to step over and around stumps, and dead branches as he walked. In the distance he saw someone, prompting him to pick up his pace. As he drew closer, he real-ized it was May. She was lying unconscious on the cold, hard ground.

"May!" Felix yelled.

He kneeled next to her lifeless body. Her entire back was stained red from the blood. He checked her pulse. It was slow, and her breaths were shallow, but she was breathing.

"Just hang on, please hang on. I cannot lose you," Felix said.

Quickly, he pulled off his coat and wrapped it around his friend. Fueled by adrenaline, he gently laid her shivering body over his shoulder and began sprinting back towards his own home. The journey back to his house felt like an eternity. Time passed slower and slower with each step towards refuge. Felix's body was numb but pulsating with adrenaline as his thin hand finally grasped the doorknob.

"Dad? Dad!" Felix yelled.

Royce rushed into sight. He was standing at the top of the stairs. His breaths were labored, Felix must have startled him.

"What is it?" Royce asked.

Felix climbed the stairs and pushed past him. He made a B line for his room. His room was fair-sized. A king-sized bed sat centered in the middle of the room. Various drawings, garment designs, random animals and scenery, were messily pinned to the slate-colored walls. A mahogany bookshelf, packed with fiction stories, non-fiction guides and religious texts, was in the corner of the room. A cat, fluffy and white, lounged in the maroon fabric armchair. Its blue eyes squinted open as Felix ran in.

"Dad get in here, please, hurry," Felix says.

Cautiously, he placed May down on his bed. Her pale skin and blonde hair were a stark contrast to the deep blue quilted bedding.

"I don't know what to do. I found her like this in the woods. She has been beaten badly, she's unconscious, and oh God she's so cold," he said.

Tears were streaming down his face. Royce rushed over. Felix drew the coat back, revealing the slashes across May's back.

"All right, calm down. I need you to focus. Go get a bucket of water and a towel for me. I am going to clean these wounds. While I do this, go get some clean cloth to wrap her back in, a shirt, and plenty of blankets," Royce said.

Reining his nerves in, Felix did as instructed. He brought his father the water and towel, fetched a cloth, a shirt and began stockpiling blankets at the foot of the bed. Royce worked carefully, caressing the lacerations with the damp towel. Several of the cuts released fresh blood which mixed in with the water and thinned out. Felix assisted him in tightly binding her torso in a soft cloth. The pair then slipped her arms through the shirt and buttoned it up. Gently, Felix bundled her in the blankets he brought, hoping to bring her warmth. Royce left the room to dump the, now dirty, water from the bucket and rinse the towel. When he returned, he saw Felix, now wearing a coat, grab his rifle.

"Son, what on earth are you doing?" Royce asked.

His expression was disapproving, he must have already known the answer.

"I am going to finish this once and for all."

"Finish what? Are you mad?"

"I am going to kill him Father. John will be dead. This is the last time he will ever hurt her. He will never lay another twisted finger on her again."

Felix trekked down the wood-covered steps. Royce was hot on his heels.

"Do you want to go to jail? This is madness, I cannot allow you to do this."

Royce grabbed his son by the shoulders and shook him gently. Felix pushed him roughly, causing him to stumble. Hatred burned in his eyes.

"I DON'T CARE! DON'T YOU UNDERSTAND? I love her. With every fiber of my body, I love this girl. And I cannot sit around and let him abuse her any longer. If you try and stand in my way, I will go through you. You cannot stop me."

Felix charged towards the door. Royce grabbed the back of his coat, making him pause.

"Wait. Son, please! Let me go with you. I can help you."

"How?"

Skepticism plagued Felix's face.

"I am going to help you make this look like a suicide."

"A suicide? Give me a break," Felix said.

He turned and reached for the knob. His father slammed his hand against the wood. Hot air escaped Felix's lips as his eyes locked with Royce's.

"Son, please, be rational! John has a small pistol he keeps in the kitchen cabinet for emergency purposes. If you use that to shoot him the sheriff will believe he shot himself."

"How am I exactly supposed to get that gun?"

"I will distract him while you go into the kitchen and grab it. While I am talking to him, you sneak behind him and shoot him."

Felix tapped his foot on the plush carpet. The room was silent, but the tension could be cut with a knife.

Having Dad there could make things messy... but, he has never let me down before. Felix closed his eyes and rubbed his eyebrows together.

"All right," Felix said.

He propped the rifle up against the wall. Royce released a small sigh of relief before quickly putting on a coat of his own and exiting the back of the tailor shop with his son in tow. The two made the long walk to May's farm in silence. Not further discussing the plan, not even uttering a word about the gloomy weather. The drizzle was gone, leaving a thin fog in its place. Some birds appeared on the overhanging branches, but their chirps were mute. By the time they arrived at the property John was sitting outside, bottle in hand.

John was a shadow of the man he once was. The hardships of farming and years of alcohol abuse had taken their toll on him physically and mentally. John was an average-sized man, not too short nor considered very tall. He was of hefty build, and even in his altered state, he was strong as he was round. His chocolate-colored hair was thin and riddled with bald spots, his face was wrinkly, and his hands were as rough as a cob. His mustache, the only thick hair on his body minus his eyebrows, covered his upper lip but could not hide the few brown and yellow teeth he still possessed. John's wild, brown eyes were permanently bloodshot.

"How-dy t-the-re friend-d," John said.

His breath was overpowering with the fumes of whiskey.

"Hello John, can we talk? I need an increase of wool for a small project I am doing," Royce said.

Felix stood behind, his blood boiling underneath his pale complexion.

"S-ure, come-come on in fe-llas," he said.

John stumbled into the house and walked to the living room. Royce glanced at his son, who quickly nodded and parted to the kitchen. Felix shook with rage and anticipation as he opened drawers and cabinet doors, searching for the gun. Behind most of the tan wood were dishes, pans, silverware and a few pieces of molded bread. Felix heard his father holding a conversation with John, making small talk about business. He slipped his dirty hands through cracked dishes, and under utensils to no avail.

"Dammit," he whispered.

Suddenly, he realized it had been hiding in plain sight. Next to the sink, the pistol sat, if it had been a snake it would have bit him. Felix gingerly brushed the gun with his fingers before he picked it up. He popped open the chamber and saw four bullets.

"How mu-ch more are-are you need-in'?" John asked.

Royce sat down opposite to him on the faded yellow sofa. His hands, slightly wrinkled from old age but not as weathered as a man working a ranch, were nervously quivering in his lap. Felix entered the room, ungraceful with movements comparable to a rabid dog. He pointed the pistol at John's head.

"You ass-wipe, you are going to hell for everything you put May through," Felix said.

John busted out into laughter, spit spewed from between his chapped lips, his hand slapped his own knee.

"Are y-you kid-din' me boy? What's a pussy like you do-ing with my gun?" he asked.

Felix was unwavering in his position. John set the whiskey bottle down at his feet and rose.

"Boy, put t-that down be-fore you hu-rt yourself," he said.

POP! POP! Felix greedily pulled the trigger, releasing two bullets from the chamber and into John's head. Brain matter and blood spewed out and splattered across the wall. The drunken man fell to the floor like a limp rag doll. A blood pool began forming around his body. He twitched until all the life has been drained.

Felix's face was spotted with John's blood. There was madness in his eyes as spat out some blood that had slipped past his lips. The taste was sour, like the poor soul that lay in a crumpled heap before him. His face was frozen as the images of John's final moments replayed over and over again in his mind. Felix's hand was still tightly clenching the murder weapon. Royce pried the gun from his son and wiped it with his coat, before he slid it into John's hand. Felix's body was trembling, prompting Royce to gently grab him by the shoulders.

"Look at me son and listen to what I have to say," Royce said. His voice was stern and cold, enough to pull Felix back into reality.

"We are going home. You are going to look after that girl. Tomorrow morning, I am going to come back here and 'find the body'. I will go to the sheriff that is staying in the inn and tell him. He's going to come back here and walk around and investigate things. He will definitely come and question May and eventually you. You were not here. I was not here. You went and found the girl, brought her home and stayed by her little side the entire night. Do you understand me? You can NEVER tell anyone, not even May, what happened here. Do you understand?"

Felix blinked, the words slowly sank in. A frown appeared on his thin lips.

"What? I cannot tell May? What about after the sheriff concludes it was a suicide?" he asked.

His father, still gripping him by the shoulders, gave him a harsh shaking.

"DID YOU NOT HEAR ME SON? I said NEVER. Not after the investigation, not next week, not next year or even ten years from now. NEVER. You must take this to your grave."

Felix released a sigh, his eyes fell to the bloodied wood floor. Never in his life had he ever kept a secret from May, much less told her even a white lie.

"Okay... I understand. I promise I will not breathe a word of it to anyone, Father."

Felix stands up from the couch, shaking his head at the memories from that night. He turns and faces the wall, tracing his fingers against where the bloody bits once stuck. It did not matter that the wall had been painted immediately after the incident or even that the furniture has been replaced. He would not, no he could not, forget the imagery from that night. He did not regret his actions against her father, but sometimes wonders what would have happened if he had told

May. Felix walks into the kitchen, picking up the knife. The only light of the hour is provided by the stars, as the moon is hidden amongst the endless darkness, but it's enough to see the wooden handle. He would not need the light anyway, his hands tracing the engrained pattern bring the familiar image to his mind. Felix knows this knife. He has held it before.

7 |

Chapter 7

With each passing day the sun's rays seem to burn brighter and hotter. With Felix by her side, May feels a little bit more at ease. She's able to concentrate on her chores, and rest peacefully knowing she's not alone. His shenanigans and upbeat personality also help her to not worry about Clint. Although she worries less, she cannot but help miss him more. His blue eyes, soft chuckles, cracked hands and sweet kisses haunt her dreams. Clint has taken half, if not more, of her heart with him. The half he left behind throbs endlessly, longing to be reunited with the other piece of its puzzle.

It's a Thursday afternoon, it has been almost a fortnight since Clint's departure, and May is sitting in the tailor shop while Felix works. Although Felix's definition of work is quite different from most, as he takes every task with great leisure. His workdays involved socializing with customers, hemming and adjusting garments, but mostly he spends his time sketching out ideas for clothes. Felix's passion is in the designing, but he leaves his father to handle the majority of the actual construction of the clothing articles. It's unspoken, but a guaranteed future, that someday Felix will inherit the shop from Royce. Felix could handle the business if it were handed to him today, but he would rather work under his father as long as possible. Not because he's not ready, but because he's still immature and distracted by the world around him.

The air in the shop is thick and muggy. Large pine trees, planted many years ago, graciously offer shade to the building; however, in the summertime even the shade cannot repel the sun's ruthless heat. May fans herself with one of Felix's sketches, trying to make up for the lack of wind. It's in vain; her body continues to produce more sweat. Staring at the ceiling, her eyes follow the movement of the boards that decorate the ceiling. The wood is stained, appearing more orange than natural or fresh-cut pieces. Suddenly, her thoughts of heat and boredom are interrupted by shouting in the distance. While the voices are loud enough to be heard, the words are muffled and difficult to make out. Curious, May gets up and Felix meets her in front of the door. Without saying a word, they look at each other and exit the shop to see if they can find where the ruckus is coming from.

They are met in the street by familiar faces of other townspeople. It's not unusual for everyone to gather when something seems amiss, considering that Pine Valley is a quiet, calm place to live. As they walk towards the butcher shop, the voices grow louder and louder.

"CATTLE DON'T JUST DISAPPEAR! WHAT DID YOU DO WITH THEM, BRIAN?" one of the voices shouts.

May freezes. The familiarity of the voice pushes her to run towards the shop and through the bystanders. Even though she already knows it's him, May still feels stunned seeing Clint standing in the street facing Brian. Clint's stance exudes anger as he furrows his brow and tightly clenches his fists. He looks ready to lunge at the butcher with a drop of a hat. In contrast, Brian looks more confused than angry; however, with each person drawing close to the quarrel he begins losing his patience.

"I already told you, I DID NOT TAKE ANY OF YOUR COWS," Brian says.

The large man crosses his arms, bulking up his stance as May watches dumbfounded. Felix pushes through the crowd and grabs May's shoulder. The pair's eyes meet, his mirror the look of horror her eyes hold. Not sure what to do, but worried about the two men engaging in a physical fight, May steps forward. Clint is so focused on Brian he does not realize she's there until she calls his name softly. Clint quickly averts his eyes from Brian to May, then back to Brian. His posture relaxes slightly, and he lets out a large sigh.

"I am done, I quit. Find someone else to screw over," Clint says. His voice is barely audible to the small audience that has gathered.

"We have a partnership, a contract, you CANNOT quit!" Brian shouts.

It's already too late. Clint has made up his mind. Turning his back to the large butcher, Clint waves for May to follow and begins walking to his horse. May shoots a pardoning glance at Felix, and follows Clint over to Moon. They leave the crowd to disperse and the angry oaf to simmer.

"I am sorry, this is not the reunion I was hoping for," Clint says.

His face still flushed from anger, as he pulls May up behind him in the saddle. May puts her arms around his waist and squeezes him as tightly as she can before she lays her head on his shoulder.

"It's okay, honestly I am just happy you are back. I really missed you," she says.

Due to his adrenaline still pumping, his body is radiating more heat than usual. His heart feels like it's going to beat right out of his chest. Even Moon picks up on the energy, swishing her tail and evolving her walk into more of a high-stepping dance. Not wanting to push him, May keeps her questions bottled up inside.

"I trusted him to look after my place for me and he cheated me," he says.

May pulls her head up, a hollow feeling growing in her stomach.

"What did he do?" she asks.

"I got back late last night, it was too dark to see if anything was amiss. Which, in reality, I was not worried about..."

"Go on," May encourages.

"When I got up this morning I wanted to come and see you bright and early, but I had to check on the herd first. Just to make sure they were fine. Almost immediately, I noticed I was a few head short. It's not just random cattle missing, both my bulls and eight of my cows had vanished. The calves were left behind, wailing in vain for their mothers to return. My first thought was to check the fence. I probably spent a good two hours, at least, going up and down the fence-line, looking for a break. There was nothing, nothing was bent, not even a gap a newborn calf could fit through. I may be perceived as a dumb rancher to some, but I know when I have been played a fool. A man I thought I could trust, my fucking partner at that, stole part of my herd. The calves he left are too young to be on their own and are going to die, and until I get another bull my production is halted."

"Why would Brian do that? Especially when you are gone for something business related. He must be as crazy as Nina said. I am sure you heard rumors about how Brian's last partnership ended. Regardless, I am sorry, I should have checked on your place. It was just I know you said it was handled, and coupled with everything that happened to me..."

"WAIT. What happened? Are you okay?" Clint asks.

"Don't worry — I am fine, or at least I am now. Someone came on my farm and slaughtered all my chickens. Every one of them. They also had the audacity to leave the knife they used stuck outside my door."

"I should have never left. If I stayed my cattle would still be here and you would not have been alone."

"You did not have a choice, and I was not alone. Felix came and helped me clean up the farm... and then he stayed with me. He has been sleeping on the couch and keeping me busy."

"I am sure he *loved* that."

Clint rolls his eyes.

"Do not give me that. You know it's not like that. He's a friend, my best friend, and nothing more," May says.

"I know what the relationship is as well as you do, it's *him* that I worry about. Could you call it a coincidence that I am not here, and something goes awry, leaving him to pick up the pieces?"

"Felix and I already had that talk, remember? He knows where I stand and accepts it. Felix just said he would be here for me if I needed him. When I needed him, he came, that is all. Why would he go to the trouble of murdering my hens if he just wanted to spend time with me? Felix cares enough about me not to do anything that would scare, or harm me... he did not kill the sheep or take my dogs either. Before you go on placing blame come and see the knife for yourself."

"All right... alright. I'll admit it, you know him better than me," Clint says.

The couple ride in silence the rest of the way to May's farm. The sun is beating down harshly on their backs. Sunflowers gently sway as a weak breeze moves through the countryside. Grasshoppers are lunging in different directions, hoping to avoid the horse's hooves from crashing down on them. The entrance to her farm is quiet, absent of the chickens' cooing that usually greets visitors. May slides off the back of Moon before Clint leads the steed to the barn. As he unsaddles, May goes into her house to get the knife.

She crosses into the kitchen and pauses. The knife is lying out on the counter. It does not matter how many times she attempted to wash it, the blade is still tinted a soft red. May sighs. She picks it up and walks into the living room where Clint meets her with a curious pose.

"So, this is it?" he asks.

Gently he takes the knife from her hand. She nods and steps back, watching him as he looks it over. From the stained blade to the intricate wooden handle, his eyes sweeping over every detail.

"Any ideas?" May asks.

"I bet, gauging by this pretty handle here, it's part of a set. Also, by the faded pattern of the wood, it has been well used prior to this," Clint says.

"So... if we were to, hypothetically speaking, find someone who owned the other pieces of the set, we would have the culprit?"

"I reckon so, but if they are smart, they would have discarded the rest of them or..."

"Or hid them away somewhere..."

"Exactly. It would be near impossible to find, unlike..." Clint pauses.

He begins to pace slowly in front of May. The thought in his head seems to transfer to hers.

"Unlike your cows," she whispers.

Clint stops pacing and looks at her, rubbing the back of his head.

"Hiding a knife set, easy; however, hiding two bulls and eight cows is not. They can be put in a barn or turned loose on acreage, but they still will have my brand," he says.

May pictures his herd mixed in with Brian's. Clint's brand, a backwards 'C' connected with an 'L' with a curved line under the letters, is visible on the left hip of all his cattle.

"There is one problem with your theory. If Brian took your animals, there is a high probability that they are disposed of. He could have moved them during the night and slaughtered them for their meat and then burnt the hides to hide the brand," she says.

May is probably giving Brian more credit and intelligence than he actually possesses.

"Good point, but if he burned the hides there would be some sort of evidence."

"Right, but does not he own over fifty acres?" she asks.

May goes over to the fabric couch and collapses into the seat cushion. Clint follows, abandoning the knife on the end table.

"Yeah, I get that it would be hard to find, unless he got lazy or cocky about it. We both know his attention span is shorter than the length of a fly's body. I know his schedule, when he's home on his ranch and when he's at the shop. We could comb over the land in the afternoon when he's at the shop, and then check the slaughterhouse during the night when he's in bed. In and out, no issues as long as we keep quiet and out of sight."

"Still would be hard for two people, unless..."

"Do not even suggest it May," Clint says.

"What? Three would be better than two, and I know Felix would help. We would be able to fan out more, and perhaps cover more land in a shorter amount of time," she suggests.

"The more people we involve, especially a loudmouth such as Felix, the more likely we would get caught."

"Come on Clint, give him a chance. I promise he will not screw us over."

"And what if he does? What then?"

"Then he will be cut out of our lives like a weed sliced from a flower garden. I will not ask for any more forgiveness or give him any more chances. But I know he will not do that. I promise," she says.

May put her hands on his shoulders and gently squeezes them. Clint sighs, lowering his forehead so that it touches hers.

"Okay," he whispers.

May starts to rise from the couch, but Clint latches onto her arm.

"Where do you think you are going?" he asks.

May, slightly stunned, stops and allows him to pull her back down.

"I... I was going to tell Felix about the plan. So, we could do it tomorrow or soon," she says. Her voice barely rises above a whisper.

Clint shakes his head no, smiling softly, and pulls her into an embrace.

"I just got back, love. You ain't going anywhere for a while," he says.

She relaxes into his body. He wraps his arms around her. She releases a sigh as she lays her head against his chest. His heartbeat echoes in her ears.

"I missed you," she says.

Clint caresses her forearm. He rests his chin on the top of her head.

"I missed you too," he says.

The sun has already gone down for its slumber and the moon had taken its shift. The wind picks up, gently blowing the crunchy leaves from tree limbs and onto the ground while owls coo in the distance. A soft knock is heard at the door, waking May from her brief nap. She looks to Clint. His eyes are still shut. He's probably pretending to be asleep. May rises from the couch, leaving the thin afghan Felix has been sleeping under, draped over Clint. Her hand hesitates over the doorknob, unready to dive back into reality and the problems that encase her.

"It's me," the voice says.

Recognizing Felix's voice from the other side of the door, May willingly opens it.

"Hi, sorry, I wasn't expecting anyone," she says.

May runs her fingers through her hair, a feeble attempt to untangle it, and casts her eyes to the ground.

"Right, I just came to get my stuff since he's back and all," he says.

Clint stands up. He stretches his arms. His half-unbuttoned shirt is poorly tucked into his unzipped pants. Felix bites his lip.

"I'll be in and out in no time," Felix says.

"Actually, we need to talk to you about something. Would you mind sitting down?" May asks.

"I guess," he says.

She guides him into the kitchen. Felix flips a chair around and sits down, resting his arms on the back. Clint follows. May takes a seat, while he leans against the wall, arms crossed, apparently still not on board with involving Felix.

"So, this morning when we saw... well I guess I should start with earlier in the morning. When Clint got back, he found that his two bulls and eight of his cows were gone. The fence wasn't broken anywhere, no gaps, it was not even slightly leaning," May says.

Clint uncrosses his arms and sighs.

"Therefore, someone had to have taken them. Brian was the one looking after his herd while he was gone. This morning, Clint confronted him, but it was to no avail. He denied any involvement," she says.

"So that is what all the commotion was about this morning?" Felix asks.

His eyes travel from May to Clint.

"Correct. After I informed Clint about the situation we had here, he had a... I don't think it's stupid, erm... not smart either, but definitely not safe idea."

"Which is what? And what does this have to do with me?" he asks.

"Well... we are going to go search Brian's property when he's not home, to see if we can find the cows, or at least any evidence to prove that they were there at some point in time. It's a large plot of land, you know, for two people to investigate. So... I suggested a third person to help, that person... being you," she says.

Felix sits silent, processing his friend's words as well as probably picturing the three of them at the property in his mind. Clint steps forward after what seemed like a few minutes of silence, but in reality, had been only a couple of seconds.

"You don't have to help. In fact, I'm not really sure I want your help anyway. All I care about is that you keep your trap shut about what we're about to do," Clint says.

"As much as I don't like you, this involves my friend. And I don't want to see anything bad happen to her, so yes, I'm going to help," Felix says. His expression is cold as he speaks, but softens as he looks to May.

"Can you be ready tomorrow?" she asks.

Felix nods, spreading a smile across her face. Clint steals an open chair and joins them at the table.

"Brian leaves his farm at around two every day to go work in the shop. He stays there until ten at night, sometimes later, before heading home. He will eat a late dinner and then go to bed. Annabelle once told me he gets up around five in the morning, sometimes sleeps in late but only if he's drunk. At three o'clock in the afternoon tomorrow, we meet here, at May's house. That gives Brian an extra hour and a half to be gone, by the time we walk over," Clint says.

May pushes her hair behind her ears.

"We search every nook and cranny of that property until we find something or the sun sets. Once it's dark, we move to the slaughterhouse. It's right behind the house he shares with Annabelle, meaning we will have to be quiet... also, we will need to be out of there before morning. We cannot, I repeat, we cannot get caught. Are you both sure that you want to do this with me?" he asks.

"Yes. I want to help any way I can," May says. She takes no time to answer, placing her hand gently over his.

Clint picks up her hand, pulling it to his lips and placing a kiss upon it. Felix looks at him, and then to May, then back to Clint.

"My answer is the same as hers, but don't kiss my hand. I'll be here tomorrow," Felix says.

Clint rolls his eyes.

"It's settled then. We can do this," she says.

Felix leaves the table to gather his belongings. He hugs May and nods to Clint, before heading out into the night. Clint wraps his arm around May as the two of them watch him walk farther and farther away until he completely disappears into the darkness.

8

Chapter 8

May nervously plays with the hem of her shirt, her stomach feels empty, like a bottomless pit, as she waits for Felix and Clint. She was barely able to sleep the night before, her mind racing around the possibility of finding the cattle, and the possibility of Brian catching them on his property. Not even her morning chores could distract her enough to give her an appetite. *Get in, get out.* Keeps echoing in her mind.

The afternoon sun is ruthless, keeping even the grasshoppers from venturing out. A feeble breeze is blowing, but it does not detract from the heat. Clint and Felix arrive almost simultaneously. Clint riding Moon, Felix trotting on foot. Both men are dressed casually, cotton shirts and plain britches, not the normal attire for Felix. Clint's sweat-soaked shirt clings to his body, appearing as if it's a second layer of skin. His black curls are flat against his head. Felix is also drenched in sweat, what can be seen of his chest gleams from moisture.

"You actually showed up," Clint says. His tone is dry with disappointment.

Felix wipes his forehead, red from the heat and damp with sweat, before casting a glare towards him.

"Come on guys, please don't start this. We have a job to do," May says.

Clint dismounts Moon, and walks to May, giving her a wet kiss on her cheek.

"All right," he says.

He leads the horse to her barn, leaving the two friends alone. Felix shades his eyes with his hand, looking out towards the empty coop.

"It's a lot quieter without your hens around," he says.

May ignores his attempt at small talk. Her mind is still adrift, unable to hide the uneasiness on her face.

"There's still time to change your mind if you want. If Clint really cares about you, he'll understand," Felix says.

"Are you saying this for me, or yourself?" she asks.

He releases a sigh and shrugs his shoulders. Clint walks back out, his eyes travel from May to Felix and then back to her.

"It's time," he says.

They walk in silence, making the walk seem even longer than it is. The dirt road is lined with trees whose branches overhang the path. Clint stops them at a barbwire fence with wood posts. Weeds and tall yellowing grass occupy the fenced land. A herd of black cows can be seen in the distance. A hand painted sign nailed to the fence reads:

"No trusspassing"

Felix covers his mouth with his hand, trying to buffer his chuckles.

"All right. We have a little over fifty acres here to search. We need to divide and conquer in order to search every area. This is the main section with his cattle. It's about forty of his acres. The next section of about ten or so acres has the barn attached to a slaughterhouse and then the house they live in. Remember, we should not search the slaughterhouse until after it's dark. Let's meet by the pond when the sun starts setting, it's towards the south side of the pasture, you can't miss it," Clint says.

"All right, I will walk down the road a bit and search this far side. I will leave you boys to fight over who gets the other areas. See you both in a few hours. Please, stay safe," May says.

She squeezes Clint's hand before slowly releasing it.

"Wait! What do we do if we find something? Or something goes awry?" Felix asks.

"Can you whistle?" Clint asks.

Felix nods but May shakes her head.

"Hmm... all right, May take this," Clint says.

He retrieves a worn white handkerchief from his back pocket and hands it to May.

"If you find something, mark it with this. Then come find one of us and we can go back to it. If Felix or I find something we will whistle," he says.

May rubs the handkerchief with her fingers before sliding it into her own pocket. Her heart is racing.

"Don't worry. We have this planned out perfectly. And if someone fails to show up at sunset we will not leave, not even you Felix, until we find them," Clint says.

His words are a slight comfort to May, but not enough to slow her heart rate. Clint turns his back to May and starts walking up the fence line. Felix mouths 'good luck' to her before climbing over the barbwire and into the pasture.

May walks down along the fence line for about fifty feet or so before deciding to wade into the sea of grass. The grass reaches slightly above her knees in most places, almost to her fingertips in other places. Her eyes scan the area, trying to digest every single detail, down to the smallest blade of grass. A stray cow, covered in flies, nervously eyes her as she approaches. She circles the animal. Its black hide is free from Clint's brand or any identification for that matter. Pressing forward she walks towards another cow, it snorts at her and tosses its head. Unlike the previous beast, this one has two good-sized horns and on closer inspection is a bull. The bull paws at the ground, spewing snot from its flared nostrils.

"You have got to be kidding me," she says.

No sooner had the words escaped her lips did the animal start barreling towards her. Rocking back on her heels she starts sprinting deeper into the thick grass. Adrenaline fuels her veins, pushing her to run as fast as she can. Suddenly she feels two points in her back, thrusting her forward. May's body is flung into the top string of the barbwire fence, momentum sends her out of the pasture and face first into a hard patch of dirt.

Her head spinning, May manages to pull herself up to a sitting position. Dirt is dusted on her pants and now torn shirt. Her forearms are scratched, bleeding lightly. A faint pain surges through her arm, soreness budding in her bones.

"Dammit," she whispers.

May runs her hand through her hair, looking up to the pale blue sky. It's cloudless. A honeybee buzzes by her ear, pulling her attention to the ground. In front of her is the modest home inhabited by Annabelle and Brian. The wood exterior of the home is painted white, but it's peeling and in need of a fresh coat. Flowerbeds, manicured and well-kept unlike the pastures, line the sides of the house. About twenty feet behind their house is the slaughterhouse. An old Percheron, droopy-eyed and slightly overweight, grazes in front of the worn-down building.

The grey-tinted building is ghastly to look at, but is captivating and alluring. May rises to her feet and walks towards the building. Her hand brushes the twin entry doors, one of the doors is slightly ajar. A putrid odor, a mixture of rotting animal hides and blood, seeps out from the opening.

"We should not search the slaughterhouse until after it's dark," Clint's words echo in her mind, halting her movements.

A peculiar noise emerges: a rhythmic stomping against the grass. May's body freezes, her insides feel hollow. The draft horse nickers, and the soft sound of stomping grass begins growing louder.

"Ma, you 'round here?" a husky voice asks.

Brian. Her spine tingles. There is nowhere for her to hide, except, inside the slaughterhouse. May swallows her breath and carefully pulls the door open, but even with her gentlest effort it releases a loud screech. Her eyes struggle to adjust to the poorly lit interior. Light peeks in from cracks in the wooden boards, and slits in the roof. Flies mass around hanging remnants of cattle carcasses. Their buzzes are deafening. Straining her eyes, May sees a large covered wagon in the corner. This is the wagon Brian uses to tow the cow carcasses to the butcher shop. She rushes to the cart, pulling herself up into the cargo area. It's empty minus a thick layer of straw. She burrows herself as deeply under the stiff, gold grass as she can. A screech signals Brian entering the slaughterhouse.

"Ma? Ma is that you?" Brian asks.

May holds her hand over her mouth, her fingers dig into her cheekbones. Her heart is pounding. Brian pulls a lantern from the wall and lights it. He tosses the match onto the dirt floor and crushes it under his boot. Brian shuffles through the musty building. His breaths are heavy. He holds the lantern up to the wagon. His hand grabs at the straw. *Clint I'm sorry. I'm so stupid. I didn't listen.* A tear slips down May's cheek. She's quivering with fear. *Brian is slow, not blind, it's only a matter of time before he finds me.* The door screeches again. She holds her breath and closes her eyes.

"Clint? What the hell are you doing here?" Brian asks.

"I needed to talk to you about yesterday. You weren't at the shop, so I came here," Clint says.

May opens her eyes.

"You've got some nerve," Brian says.

"Coming from the man that stole my cattle? That's rich," he says.

Brian grunts.

"I already told you—"

"Stop. I'm not here to argue with you. You owe me money from last month. Annabelle said she accidentally shorted me," he says.

"She never said anything to me, but I guess I can check the books."

"Math isn't exactly your strong point. I don't trust you to look alone. I want to see the records for myself," Clint says.

"Fine, come on then," he says.

Brian sets the lantern on a table and the they leave.

May takes a deep breath. Her body is damp with sweat. She slips out of the wagon and brushes the straw from her arms. *Thank you, Clint.* She walks to the lantern, still lit with its flame dancing beneath the glass. The table where it sits is dark with dried blood. An unorganized variety of meat hooks, knifes and chains are on top of it. Approaching footsteps send May under the table. She grips the splintered wooden legs. Spiders flee from the cobwebs above her head.

"Psst, May? May are you still in here?" Felix asks.

He pokes his head in through the ajar door. May sighs, placing her hand over her heart.

"I'm over here," she says.

Felix walks in, swatting away a fly.

"Damn, it's disgusting in here," he says.

She crawls out from underneath table. He offers his hand and helps her stand up.

"Thank you. How did you guys know I was in here?" she asks.

"I saw you running so I hollered at Clint. We couldn't see what you were running from or where you were going but thought it could've been from Brian. Guess we were right."

"Actually, I was running from a bull. Then I heard footsteps... so I hid in here. If Clint hadn't come when he did, Brian would've found me."

His eyes fall to her arms.

"What happened? Are you okay?" he asks.

"I'm fine, just hit the barbwire fence."

"We'll have to clean that up when we get back. Now come on, we need to get out of here before he comes back. If he figures out Clint was bullshitting, he might suspect something's up."

May nods. He gently cuffs her wrists and leads her out of the slaughterhouse. The afternoon sun is harsh, but the air is less humid than it was inside the building.

"We need to go out through the back," he whispers.

"What about Clint?" she asks.

"He said he's going to meet us back at your house, but we have to go now," he says.

May nods reluctantly. She does not want to leave him but knows the longer they linger the higher the chance his actions will be in vain.

The back of the property is as unkept as the rest. Old plows, horse harnesses, wagon wheels and troughs are littered about. Mesquite trees, some around three feet tall with others almost full grown, are thickly braided into the ground. They get thicker and taller the closer it gets to the back of the property line. The mesquite trees are almost more prevalent than the pines. Their thorns prick at them as they walk through.

The barbwire fence, rusted and loosely tied to posts, is a welcome sight. Felix holds down the top wire while May steps over. A feeling of relief washes over her as her shoe meets the yellowed grass of the vacant property. May and Felix walk in silence. Birds chirp overhead, rabbits scatter as they approach. In an opening of trees, a modest house sits. Next to it is an old, rotting barn.

"Is... is this Jason's property?" May asks.

They stop walking. Felix looks at her and scratches the back of his head.

"Jason who?" he asks.

"Brian and Annabelle's old business partner. The one that disappeared," she says.

"That guy... I didn't know his name, but it might be. He disappeared? I thought he left town?"

"I did too, until I talked to Nina. Long story short, something bad happened between him and Brian."

May trots over to the house and Felix follows close on her heels. Like the barn, it's in poor shape. The windows are cracked and busted open.

"Wait, May. Should we be doing this?"

"Is it any worse than snooping around on Brian's property?"

Felix opens his mouth to argue but stops. He probably knows she's right. May follows the wraparound porch to the front of the home. The door has fallen off its hinges. Rain and other weather has tormented the interior. It reeks of mold. The furniture is set up as if it was not abandoned, but instead the owner was planning on returning. Two rocking chairs are placed adjacent to each other in the living room. A coffee table, weighted with a candle and chipped coffee mug, sits in the center of the room.

"This is creepy," Felix says.

The floorboards squeak underneath their feet. Heavy dust hangs in the air. The ceiling is rotting, plaster is drooping down in several places. A scrawny black cat hisses at them and flees out a window. Felix shudders and rubs his forearms.

"Felix... if you were going to do something criminal, would you hide evidence on your property?" she asks.

"No... why...? Oh, I see where you're going," he says.

May steps over a fallen lantern, its glass is shattered across the floor. She tries to open a door into a side room. It does not budge. Felix grabs the knob, roughly yanking on it. Still, it refuses to move.

"Hang on, I bet there's a tool or something around here I can use to pry it open," he says.

May watches him walk off before turning to another door. It's cracked open. Her hand hesitates over the knob. *There has to be something around here.* A loud humming is being emitted from behind the door, similar to what she heard in the slaughterhouse. A foul smell hits her as she pulls it open. The room is small and dark. Tattered curtains block the sunlight. A shadowed silhouette is slumped in a corner against the wall. Slowly, May approaches it. Her hand wavers by the curtains, hesitating before pulling them down. Her mouth falls open. The light reveals the thing in the corner is actually a rotting human corpse. The corpse is riddled with bullet holes, from its thin torso to its balding skull. Its brown fingers are wrapped around the handle of a rusted pistol.

The grey walls are darkened with dried blood. Decayed pieces of flesh are splattered across the room. Maggots squirm in and out of the holes littering the body. May goes to take a step back but slips on the curtain and falls. Flies scatter as her bottom hits the wood-paneled flooring. Her hands shake as she pulls them up, foreign matter and dead insects are stuck to her palms. She gags, struggling to swallow the growing lump in her throat. Tears fill her eyes. Nothing could have prepared her for this. *This is different. It's not a sheep, or poultry, but a human. I can't do this.* She manages to push herself a few feet back, but her legs feel too weak to stand up on.

"F-Felix, get in here," May says.

Felix rushes in the doorway, stopping next to May.

"Oh shit," he says.

Felix grabs her by the arms and pulls her up. Her entire body is quivering. He clasps her face with his hands, bringing her eyes to his.

"May? May are you okay?" he asks.

She blinks twice before slowly nodding. Gentle tears are streaming down her cheeks.

"Take a few deep breaths," he says.

May breathes in the foul air, releasing it with a cough.

"All right, come on. You don't need to see this," Felix says.

He pulls her face into his chest. Her crying intensifies. The wetness of her tears bled through Felix's shirt. His eyes linger on the corpse as he caresses her back.

"Please... take me home," she whispers.

May sits on the couch in her living room, her body is still shaking. Felix brings her a glass of water.

"Here, drink this," he says.

She pulls the glass to her lips. Her trembling fingers make the water slosh out onto her face. Felix grits his teeth. He takes the glass from her and places it on the coffee table.

"Are you sure I can't make you something to eat?" he asks.

May shakes her head. She runs her fingers through her hair. Felix sits halfway on the couch, seemingly prepared to jump up and catch her. Her eyes fixate on him. He seems unmoved by the corpse.

"... How are you handling this so well?" she asks.

Felix opens his mouth as if to say something, but hesitates. He strokes his chin. Uneasiness lingers in his eyes.

"Felix?"

"Uh, it's... nothing. I just was expecting something bad. I wasn't surprised, that's all."

May shakes her head.

"I know you better than that. Tell me the truth," she says.

Felix takes a deep breath; his eyes avoided her gaze. May turns to him, placing her hands on his knees.

"What is it?"

He puts his hand over hers and sighs.

"This wasn't the first time I've seen a dead body. I mean, this guy has been dead longer, but still," he says.

May's eyes widen. Her hands feel clammy.

"What are you talking about? When? Why haven't you told me before?"

"I wanted to tell you May, I really did."

"Then why didn't you?"

"Because my father... he told me I couldn't."

"Because Royce? You didn't tell me because your dad told you not to? Are you serious? How dumb do you think I am to believe a lie like that?"

May yanks her hands from under his. She stands up from the couch and crosses her arms. Felix jumps up. He clamps his hands down on her forearms.

"May, please. You don't understand. It's not like that, I'm not lying."

"Yes, you are! You know, I've never lied to you. I've always told you everything. You're like a brother to me."

His face reddens. "But I'm not your brother, and I've never wanted to be your brother!"

"Why? What's wrong with that?"

His grip tightens on her arms. Her heart rate increases. Their eyes are locked on each other. Felix pulls her against him, pressing his lips against hers. His kiss is soft like flower petals. It makes her feel relaxed. Her hands fall to her side, her body stops trembling. Felix presses for more. His kisses grow rougher. His hands slide underneath her shirt and up her back. His warmth is comforting like a blanket. She feels herself, letting go. Her hands wrap around his thin waist. It feels different. Clint's face flashes in May's mind. Her eyes open. *This is wrong.* She tries to push him away but he's holding her too tight. May panics. There is a small part of her that doesn't want him to stop. Maybe it's curiosity, she's never been kissed by anyone besides Clint, or maybe it's something more; regardless she knows she has to stop it. She bites down on his lip, drawing blood. Felix releases her and stumbles back. He places his hand on his face. He looks horrified.

"What the hell May? What are you doing?"

"Me? What about you?"

Suddenly, the front door blows open and Clint rushes in. His eyes wildly scan the room before stopping on May. He sighs, his body relaxing.

"My God, I was so worried about you," he says.

He throws his arms around May. She presses her face into his chest, her breaths are heavy. Felix rubs his temples, turning away from the couple. He slowly moves towards the door. Clint kisses the top of May's head.

"Felix?" Clint says.

"Yes?" he asks.

May refuses to look at Felix. *I can't believe he did that... or me.* She grips the back of Clint's shirt.

"Thank you for getting her back safely," Clint says.

"Yeah, sure, no problem. I'm going to go into town and talk to someone about getting a sheriff down here to take a look at that body," Felix says.

"Body?" Clint asks.

He looks from Felix to May, narrowing his brow.

"Ask May to fill you in," he says.

He briskly leaves, slamming the door as he exits. Clint turns to May. Her eyes refuse to meet his. Guilt shadows her mind.

"That was a tense reunion. Something tells me it didn't have anything to do with the body he mentioned?"

May shakes her head. Clint sits on the couch and she follows his lead. He cups her hands in his. She takes a deep breath.

"Felix kissed me."

"Are you kidding me?"

I wish I was. "No."

"That son of a bitch. No wonder he left so quickly."

Clint scratches the back of his head.

"Maybe it was my fault. We found a corpse in the house that I think used to belong to Brian's old partner, Jason. I... I didn't handle it well and I let Felix coddle me. Maybe he read more into it. I don't know."

Clint puts his arm around her shoulder, pulling her close until her head is resting on his chest. His lips linger above her hair.

"It's not your fault. I always knew he has feelings for you. He just waited for the right opportunity to take advantage of you."

She thinks of Felix. His golden hair, his soft lips, and warm skin. She knows it wasn't just him, she had let him kiss her. It didn't matter that she stopped it, she allowed it to happen in the first place, and for that, she's just as guilty as he is.

"Can we just pretend this day didn't happen and move on?"

"...You guys found a body. I don't think we can forget to-day, and I don't know if anything will be the same after this gets out, but tonight we can pretend like we're the only two people in this town. Okay?"

"Okay."

Chapter 9

Most of Pine Valley's residents are tightly packed in the town's square. Becca's father, Mark, stands in between Royce and Annabelle. He tugs at the ends of his chocolate-brown, handlebar mustache. His brow is thick with perspiration as the morning sun beats down on his back. The sweat on the top of his head has made his combover lie flat. He's over-dressed in a tan shirt with an overcoat. Annabelle is wearing a long white dress embroidered with lilac-colored flowers. Her silver hair is pulled into a tight bun. Her glasses rest on the tip of her thin nose. Royce rolls up the sleeves on his pale blue, cotton shirt. His white pants are stiff and wrinkle free. Like Mark, he's sweating profusely. May stands at the front of the crowd, her fingers are interlocked with Clint's. Felix walks up beside her.

"Did I miss anything?" he asks.

May shakes her head. The entire town has been gathered together for almost two hours now. Even the children are in attendance, although they are more concerned with playing with ladybugs and wildflowers at the square's edge. Word of mouth in a town as small as this always travels fast, but the news of the body spread like a wildfire on a dry windy day. Mark, being one of the pillars of the community, serves as a makeshift town leader and had scheduled this meeting in the late hours of the night before.

"This is a wild goose chase," Annabelle says.

"Mrs Grey, please. No one is accusing anyone of anything, we are just trying to get to the bottom of this," Mark says.

Clint steps forward, briskly dropping May's hand.

"I am. I'm accusing Brian. He stole part of my herd while I was out of town," he says.

Annabelle's wrinkled hands ball into fists.

"Clint, I do not know what you are talking about! As a partner, we never treated you wrong, yet here you stand trying to drag my son's name through the mud. Brian may not have the best social skills or manners, but he's a good person. He would never do such a thing," she says.

"What about the body? On the property behind yours? Wasn't that your last business partner? Pretty convenient after a disagreement he ended up dead," he says.

Gasps and unintelligible murmurs echo in the crowd behind him. May and Felix nervously lock eyes, but she pushes her gaze away. She still has not forgiven him for the kiss or herself for not stopping it before it happened. An awkward tension hangs in the air around them.

"How dare you! How dare you accuse my son of murder! I treated you like a second son," Annabelle says.

Before Clint can say anything else, Annabelle suddenly claws at her chest. Her face is red and strained. Several veins are protruding from her neck and forehead. She falls to the grey stone ground, convulsing. Mark throws his hand over his mouth in shock, and Royce rushes to be beside Annabelle. She stops twitching and goes limp. She isn't breathing. Royce immediately starts trying to resuscitate her with chest compressions. Nothing. He breathes into her mouth and resumes the compressions. The seconds tick by more slowly than dripping honey. Still, no change. Brian rushes up. He nearly knocks several bystanders to the ground as he plows through the crowd.

"Ma? Ma?" he says.

Royce lays two fingers on her neck, and then her wrist. His expression is grim as his eyes lock with Felix's and then Brian's. He shakes his head. *Is she... gone?* A shiver runs up May's spine. Brian falls to his knees beside his mother. His fat fingers caress Annabelle's hair. Snot oozes from his pig-shaped nose.

"Mark, clear the square. This is not a public spectacle and we need some space," Royce says.

Mark steps forward. He nervously adjusts the collar of his shirt and clears his throat.

"Citizens of Pine Valley. This meeting is adjourned... for now. Please return to your homes and places of business at once. I will be in touch with you all at a later date to resume this. Thank you," he says.

The residents are uncharacteristically silent as they dispense and shuffle away. Felix puts his hand on May's shoulder, but she shrugs it off. He grimaces, embarrassed, and turns away. May grabs Clint's arm.

"We should probably go too," she says.

Brian turns away from Annabelle and shoots a glare at Clint. He rises to his feet. His entire body is trembling.

"This... this is all YOUR fault!" Brian spits.

He tears off his blood-stained apron and takes an offensive step towards Clint. May's grip tightens around his forearm. Clint takes a deep breath.

"I know you're upset, and I get that, but this was not anyone's fault," he says.

Brian lunges. His beefy fist meets the underside of Clint's jawline with a pop, knocking him back. May, still holding onto Clint, stumbles and falls. Felix catches her before she hits the pavement.

"What the hell, Brian?" Felix asks before adding, "are you okay, May?"

She nods. Everything happened so fast. She didn't even realize she was falling until she almost hit the ground. Felix helps her stand up and pulls her away from the angry butcher.

"Brian, son, you need to calm down," Royce says.

Brian lunges again, but this time Clint is ready. He catches Brian's punch and thrusts his arm back towards him. Although Brian is heavier than Clint, weighing somewhere well over 250 pounds, he's shorter, much shorter. And where Clint has muscle, Brian has solely fat. He forcefully throws his left hand into Clint's stomach, making him wince. A scowl plagues his face. The empathy has all but evaporated from his eyes, leaving anger in its place. Clint hooks Brian under his chin and then drives his fist into his fleshy cheek.

Clint swings again, burying his knuckles into Brian's mouth. Brian falls. His head hits the pavement with a thud, knocking him unconscious.

"That's ENOUGH!" Royce says.

He throws his hands out, and steps between the two men. Clint's breaths are heavy and exasperated. Sweat sits on his brow line.

"What were you thinking? Engaging him like that? His mother just died for Christ's sake," Royce says.

"He came at me first," he says.

Clint turns away from him and walks over to May. He pulls her into a tight embrace. She buries her face in his chest. His heart is beating loudly against her ear.

"Are you okay?" she asks.

"I'm fine," he whispers.

Felix nervously looks at Brian. His round face is red from Clint's blows. A bruise is already forming on his cheek.

"He could regain consciousness at any given second. Please, get her out of here," Felix says.

"What are you going to do with him? Clint asks.

Royce and Mark exchange worried looks with each other, suggesting they had not thought about much in advance.

"I don't know. We're all in a little bit over our heads here. That's why we sent out word to the folks in Oak Ridge. Their town sheriff should be arriving some time tonight," Royce says.

"A sheriff? He probably should be locked up somewhere. You better keep him away from us until then. My patience is gone. I own quite a bit of ammunition, but I won't waste any on a warning shot. Come on, May, let's go," Clint says.

Felix watches them as they walk over to Moon. The horse's eyes are wide. Her hooves tap against the pavement uneasily as Clint climbs into the saddle. *She must be absorbing all this tension*. May sighs. He pulls her up on Moon, and turns the horse away from the town. Even with her head against his back, May can still hear his rapid heartbeat. As they ride, his body is tense and stiff, refusing to melt under her tender touch. It feels as awkward as the first time she rode with him.

"What's wrong?" she asks.

"Nothing," Clint says.

"Don't be like that, Clint. I know you. You're upset."

He shifts his body in the saddle.

"You shouldn't have been standing so close to me. You were in the way and almost got hurt," he says.

May scoffs. He grits his teeth.

"Excuse me, I was trying to stop things from escalating."

"You made it worse."

"Are you kidding me right now? I made it worse? You were the one who started arguing with Annabelle. You're probably the reason she…"

"The reason she what? Why don't you just say it. You think I'm the reason she died?"

Clint roughly pulls the horse to a stop.

"I-I didn't mean that," she says.

A few seconds of silence pass. The only audible noise is the rustling of the tree branches as the wind slips through them.

"I think you should walk the rest of the way home," he says.

May's grip around him tightens. She presses her forehead into his back.

"Clint, please! I'm really sorry, I—," he pulls her hands from around his waist, cutting her off. She goes to wrap her arms around him again, but he pushes her away.

"Don't make me tell you again," he says.

Reluctantly, May slides off the back of the horse. Her eyes are watering as she reaches for Clint's knee. His knee, along with the rest of his body, is quivering.

"Please, don't leave me like this. Things got heated and I didn't mean what I was saying… it just came out," she says.

"I'll see you later."

He kicks Moon's sides roughly. May watches helplessly as the horse picks up a brisk trot which transitions into a lope as he kicks her again. *What did I just do?* She crumbles to the ground, pressing her face into her hands. Hot tears slide down her cheeks.

May sits at her kitchen table. The table is bare minus a half-empty glass of wine. The wine itself is a deep red, and is as bitter as it's dark. Her face is stoic, but her eyes are dry and pink. It's half-past seven and she has not seen or heard from Clint since their fight. She tried to push herself to leave her home and go see him, but she could not bring herself to make it off the front porch. Although his back was to her, she cannot stop picturing the look of pain and horror on Clint's face he probably had when he processed her words.

There is a knock at the door. It's brisk, but the two knocks that follow it are timid. *Clint?* May rushes to the door, leaving her wine at the table.

"May? It's me," a voice says.

Felix.

"I don't want to talk to you right now," she says.

"I know, but we need to talk."

She walks away from the door. It creaks as it opens.

"I wanted to check up on you, make sure everything was okay, after everything that happened this morning..."

His eyes look to the kitchen, falling upon the wine glass.

"You never drink alone."

May shrugs her shoulders. "Maybe you don't know me as well as you thought. I certainly don't know you."

"Come on May don't be like that."

Felix reaches for her arm. She recoils under his touch.

"Please don't touch me."

He walks closer, pulling her around so they are face to face. His face is somber as he takes in her expression. He can tell she's been crying.

"What has happened to us? You've been so different since Clint moved here."

She scoffs. "Me? I've been different? You're the one who's changed. Suddenly it's like you're a different person. We've been fighting tenfold more than we used to, and then you kissed me..."

"You kissed me back," he whispers.

Moisture forms in her dry eyes. She nods her head.

"I did. And I'm going to have to live with that guilt."

Felix sighs.

"You shouldn't feel guilty... it was meaningless for you."

"Maybe it wasn't, and that's why I feel so terrible."

His eyes widen. "What do you mean?"

She crosses her arms. Her eyes fall to the ground

"I felt something when you kissed me. It's not the same as when I kiss Clint, but there was something there. Enough to scare me."

He takes a step closer to her.

"Why does it scare you?"

"I don't know."

"Yes, you do."

He puts his hand under her chin and pulls her face up. Their eyes meet briefly before she looks away.

"Tell me why it scares you," he says.

"Because, it didn't feel wrong. I imagined if I ever kissed anyone else it would feel like a mistake. For a split second, it felt right. It made me wonder how my life would be today if you had kissed me sooner. Would we be together? Would I still be in this God-forsaken town?"

His hand slides to her cheek.

"Maybe it's a sign, May. Maybe this is the universe's way of telling us we should be together. We could go anywhere. We could leave this place behind, like we always talked about."

She shakes her head. A tear slips down her cheek.

"You don't understand. I love Clint, with all my heart. That kiss, no matter how I felt then or now, doesn't change anything."

"What if I told you I loved you? Would that change any-thing?"

There is a soft knock. May and Felix both turn towards the door. Felix goes to the window. He draws back the curtain, just enough to peer outside.

He sighs. "It's Clint."

May looks from her friend to the door.

"May? Are you home? Will you please let me in?" he says.

"We can't leave things at this. Can you tell him to come back later?" Felix asks.

His eyes are expectant. A lump grows in her throat. The knob turns, and Clint slips in.

"Felix? What are you doing here?"

Both men look to May. She opens her mouth to speak, but her throat is dry. She turns her back to them and walks to-wards the staircase. Felix bites his lip, shaking his head in dis-belief.

"I was just leaving. Goodnight May."

Clint clicks the door shut behind Felix. She wants to turn and face him, but she can't. Not only is she scared he's going to have that same expression of sorrow that wouldn't stop re-playing in her mind earlier, she's also scared he'll know what was said between Felix and her. Somehow a simple gesture or wrong expression could give it away in an instant. Her knees feel weak. She reaches for the railing. Suddenly, his arms are around her, his chin resting on her head. His grip tightens. Warmth spreads throughout her entire body from his touch. A feeling Felix's touch has never resulted in. She feels wet drops on her hair. Tears are cascading down his face and onto her head.

"May, I'm so sorry," he whispers.

May turns to face him. His eyes are red, and bloodshot. Snot rests on his upper lip. His pained face is far worse than the one she imagined.

"I'm so sorry. I shouldn't have said what I said. I should have never left you in the middle of the road. I should have come over sooner. I'm... not good enough for you, I—"

"Shut up."

May cups his face in her hands, interrupting his stream of tears with her thumbs. Tears start slipping down her cheeks as well. He places his hands over hers.

"I love you more than anything in this world. Don't you ever say you're not good enough for me. I shouldn't have said what I did," she says.

He shakes his head.

"That's not true. I was an ass. When Brian came after me, you almost got hurt. I didn't protect you, I didn't even try," he says.

"You weren't expecting him to do that," she says.

"But I should have. I told you, I would always protect you, but when it came time for me to do that, I failed. For shit sakes, Felix was a better man to you than I was."

His words hit her stomach like a sucker punch. Clint walks away from her and slams his fist into the wall. The house rattles. May grabs his hand before he can hit the wall again.

"Stop, please," she whispers.

He falls to his knees. May kneels next to him. She places her hands on his shoulders.

"You didn't fail to protect me. The only thing you did wrong was leaving in the middle of an argument. I've never been in a relationship before, but I know that's no way to handle disagreements," she says.

"I... I don't know what I'm doing. I've cared for other girls before, but it has never been anything like this. I've never loved anyone before," he pauses, looking into her eyes, "I'm sorry. I've always dealt with problems on my own. I don't know how to do this."

May pushes his curls behind his ear.

"Please don't beat yourself up about this. I've messed up too."

Her thoughts wander to the kiss shared between Felix and herself, and the words to him she knows she can never take back. She shakes the image of her friend from her mind.

"I don't know how to do this either, but I can learn. We can learn together. We must. This is our new normal," she says.

"...So, you still want to be with me?" he asks.

"Of course, don't be silly. I love you."

Clint leans in, pressing his forehead against hers.

"I love you too," he says.

May kisses him. His lips are chapped, but they are also moist from his tears.

"I have something for you," he pauses, wiping the snot onto his sleeve, "it's outside."

He stands up, offering his hand to her. She takes it.

"Do you trust me?" he asks.

"Yes, why?"

"Close your eyes. Let me guide you."

May takes a deep breath before closing her eyes. With one hand on her waist and the other cupping her wrist, he leads her outside. The night air is cool, a reminder than summer is almost over. Crickets chirp melancholically. Clint is careful to make sure she does not slip as they step off the front porch. He guides her to the barn.

"Wait here a second," he says.

He lights a lantern and hangs it on the wall.

"Okay, you can open them now."

Standing in the stall next to Moon is a stunning, golden palomino horse. Its mane, white and flaxen, is braided and falls past its neck. Its tail is silver at the top and then darkens to a brownish blonde tip. Clint's brand, freshly done and still scabbing, is burned on its shoulder. The horse's head is delicate and feminine, marked with a thick white blaze. Its eyes are an unusual copper color.

He... bought me a horse? May covers her mouth in awe.

"What do you think? She's only three, but she has a good mind and disposition. I rode her around before I purchased her. She watches her surroundings, like a typical young horse, but she doesn't spook much. And she's really fast. Most girls like fast horses, right?"

The horse reaches her head over the stall and sniffs May's hand. May looks at the golden beauty and then to Clint. She opens her mouth, but nothing comes out. She's speechless. Clint unlatches the stall door.

"They were calling her Blondie, but you can call her whatever you want. Come here, come get a better look at her," he says.

May enters the stall. The horse eyes her while she pushes her hand underneath its fluffy forelock. The horse watches Clint as he enters the stall.

"She doesn't look like a Blondie... no, I think she should be called Starlight or Star for short. You'll have Moon and I'll have Star. Where did you get her? And when?"

"Star, huh? I like it. Suits her well."

He pats the horse's neck.

"Do you remember when I went out of town for business?" he asks.

May nods.

"I lied. It wasn't for business. It was personal. Very personal. Did you see her mane? Come here," he says.

May slips underneath the horse's neck and stands in front of Clint. He guides her hand to caress one of the long, shimmery braids. Her finger stops at the end. Something hard is entangled in the braid. *What is this?* She looks at Clint, his expression is anxious. Light sweat beads on his forehead.

"Unbraid that strand," he says.

She draws her attention back to the braid. Carefully, her fingers untwine the hair until the object slips into her hand. It's a ring. A beautiful, dainty ring. It has a gold band with a garnet gemstone resting at the top.

"What is this for?" she asks.

Clint takes a deep breath. He gets down on one knee. May's heart races.

"I love you more than anything in this world. I know I'm not perfect. No matter how hard I try not to, I will still make mistakes and sometimes I will hurt you. I cannot imagine my life without you and I hope you can't imagine your life without me. I've told you before that you are a flame, and I'm a mere wax. Wax makes candles, and candles need a flame to glow. The flame can stand and grow on its own, but the wax cannot. I need you. I promise that from this day forward, I won't abandon you when I'm upset. I won't keep my problems bottled up inside, but instead I'll allow you to help me as I always should've. May Ferrothorn, will you please marry me?"

May takes a deep breath. Tears are forming in her dry eyes.

"Stand up," she says.

A worried expression paints his face, but he stands. She throws her arms around his neck, nearly pulling him over. Her grip tightens around him like a snake coiling around its prey. A few tears slide down her cheeks. She can hear his heart beating out of his chest.

"Yes," she whispers, "I will marry you."

"Really?"

"Yes!"

He laughs, joy spreads across his face. May slides the ring onto her finger. It's a little snug, but fits. He picks her up and spins, spooking the horse.

"Careful now," she says.

He sets her down. They laugh in unison.

"I'm sorry, I'm just... so happy," Clint says.

May puts her hands on his cheeks. She leans forward, planting a kiss on his lips. He bites her lip as she pulls her face away.

"I know, I'm happy, too," she whispers.

Clint pulls her into a tight embrace. His heart is still racing.

"Would you like to go on a night ride to celebrate?" he asks.

May shakes her head.

"Really? Why not? The moon is almost full, we'd have enough light."

"I know, but I want to celebrate in a different way... come on."

Clint follows her out of the stall. May stops, facing the pile of loose hay. Her back to him, she casually separates the buttons on her thin shirt. Clint watches as the shirt falls to the dirt. He comes up behind her, and flips her around. She grips the fabric of his shirt, pulling him close to her. Her fingers tear at the buttons on his shirt until his chest is exposed. Their lips press roughly against each other. Hastily, they strip the rest of their clothes off. His warm, calloused hands grab her waist. She wraps her legs around him as he lifts her into the air. With a thud, he pushes her up against the barn wall. Her fingernails dig into his muscular back. Heat radiates off their sweaty bodies. Lust and euphoria fuel them.

Chapter 10

May sits on the fabric couch in her living room. Felix sits next to her. His hands cradle a cup of black coffee. She nervously twists the engagement ring on her finger. Her ears strain to hear the low murmurs coming from the kitchen. Inside the kitchen, Clint is talking to the sheriff, Greg Alder. The sheriff has been in town for four days now. He's tall, somewhere in his mid-thirties, with a baby face. His dark brown hair is peppered with grey.

"Are you going to the moon viewing tonight?" Felix asks.

Every year, the town gathers in the square to celebrate the first harvest moon of autumn. There is food, drinks and a small band to entertain the villagers while they interact with one another and celebrate the passage from summer into fall. As children May and Felix would attend with their fathers and everyone else at the square. When they got older, they started venturing off, sneaking wine out onto public, unoccupied land where they drank and talked about the future, how the next moon viewing would be different, but each year they held the same routine.

"I'm not going to the square. Clint and I were thinking about going to the lake."

"Oh."

Felix looks down at the coffee in his hand. It's cold and stale. May shifts uncomfortably on the couch cushion.

"I went to Annabelle's funeral."

"How was it?"

"Weird, but still sad. Brian was inconsolable. Mark and my dad had to escort him back home, which left me there alone. I had been hoping you were going to be there... we really need to talk about some things."

"I know. I just didn't think it would appropriate for me to go. I mean after all I am Clint's..." her voice trails off as Felix looks to her hand.

He briskly grabs her wrist and pulls her hand close to his face.

"Is that... an engagement ring?" he asks.

May nods. Felix takes a deep breath. Moisture is building in his eyes.

"I... was not expecting this. You agreed to marry him, even after everything that was said between us the other night?"

He brushes away a lone tear before it can slip past his cheek. A strange feeling, a mixture of sorrow and discomfort, buds in May's stomach. The seconds of silence that tick by feel more like hours. May hesitantly puts her hands over Felix's. They are trembling.

"Can you be happy for me? Please?"

Felix takes a deep breath. Another tear glides down his cheek. He opens his mouth, but before he can respond, Clint and Greg enter the living room. May pulls her hands from Felix's and rises from the couch. The sheriff adjusts his shirt collar.

"We're finished, for now. I want to thank you all for taking time out of your mornings to speak with me. Right now, this is an open investigation and I may need to talk to one of you again in the future. May, can I have one more word with you?" Greg says.

May looks to Clint. He nods, as if to say it's okay.

"Yes," she says.

She follows Greg into the kitchen. Her mind is no longer concerned with the corpse, or Brian. All she can think about is the hurt that reflected in Felix's eyes. The feeling in her stomach is gone. She just feels hollow on the inside. The kitchen table is a mess with a disheveled stack of papers covered in illegible scribbles. The knife that had been used to kill her chickens is on the edge of the table.

"Clint mentioned something about one of your sheep having its throat slit, followed by your chickens being killed several weeks later. Why didn't you mention this to me during our interview?" he asks.

She shrugs her shoulders. "I didn't think it was relevant."

"This is a murder investigation. Everything is relevant," he says.

"I'm sorry."

"It's fine. But is there anything else you failed to mention to me earlier?"

She shakes her head.

"All right, but if anything else happens, I need you to tell me."

"I will, I promise."

The sheriff gathers his papers and exits the house. Clint and May watch as he rides his black horse off her property. She lets out a deep sigh, and Clint puts his arm around her.

"I know the feeling," he whispers.

The house is quiet. Too quiet for three people to be inside. May looks over her shoulder, the couch is vacant. Her eyes scan the rest of the room. It's empty.

"W-where's Felix? He was just here."

"He left right when you went in there to speak with Greg. Said he had some things to sort out. I don't what he meant, I thought he already talked to the sheriff, but he looked like Hell."

May looks down to the ring on her finger. The sunlight catches the garnet stone, reflecting small pigments of light onto the walls. Felix's words, 'What if I told you I loved you? Would that change anything?', play over and over again in her mind.

"Did something happen while I was speaking with Greg?"

"No. We were just catching up. Please don't worry, everything is fine."

The moon is full. It's painted like a sunset with hues of pumpkin orange and golden yellow. The night air is cool, a light breeze pushes through the trees. Frogs are croaking. May and Clint are lying on a woolen blanket by the edge of the lake. Star is tied to a low-hanging tree branch. Her tail swishes as the occasional fly lands on her hip.

"This is really good exposure for her," Clint says.

"Yeah I agree. It's just a shame Moon isn't feeling well."

"I think she has a stone bruise or maybe an abscess. She just keeps giving to her front right leg. I know she hates being stalled, but she'll heal quicker if she rests."

May rolls over onto her side. Her hand rests on Clint's stomach. A smile sits on her face. Clint's eyes are fixated on the moon.

"It's really something," he says.

"Yeah it is. We could always get married at night, under a moon like this."

"Isn't that bad luck or something?"

May scoffs. "That's rain, silly. Since when do you believe in luck, anyway?"

"... Since I met you."

Her face flushes. He squeezes her hand.

"When do you want get married anyway?" she asks.

"I haven't really thought about it too much. What do you think?"

"Sometime in spring, that's when the scenery is most idealistic."

"We can do spring," he pulls her hand to his lips, "that is, if everything is calmed down around here by then."

May sighs. "Honestly, I'm afraid things will never be the same here."

She stands up and walks towards the edge of the lake. The moon's reflection glimmers off the calm water. Clint stands up and walks up behind her. He wraps his arms around her waist, resting his chin on her head.

"You know, we don't have to stay here. Shit, we don't even have to get married here. I can sell what's left of my herd, you can sell your flock, we pack up everything we care for and ride out east, maybe even west, Hell, south, or north works too, as long as I'm with you, I don't care where we end up," he says.

May turns around. Her eyes lock with his.

"D-do you mean that?"

He nods. A smile spreads across her face, and she buries her face in his chest. His tightens his arms around her.

"Just me and you," he whispers.

Felix's face flashes in her head. His eyes are red and swollen from crying. His hand weakly raises as he offers a half-hearted wave. It would probably devastate him if she left. *What about Royce? Felix isn't really alone. He stands to inherit the tailor business. He has a life in Pine Valley. He couldn't be that hurt by me leaving...*

"Do you smell that?" Clint's words interrupt her thoughts.

She pulls her face up from his chest. *Smoke?*

They both look to the sky. A thin, wispy haze is now present above the tree line.

"Now that you mention it..."

Star snorts. Her eyes are wide. Clint walks to the horse and strokes her neck.

"It must be close, we should go check it out, just to make sure everything is okay."

May nods. He begins to untie the horse, while she rolls up the blanket. Clint fastens it to the saddle. May steps up, extending her hand to Clint. A grin spreads across his face.

"You're enjoying this too much."

"Maybe a little."

He pulls himself up and secures himself behind her and the saddle. His thick arms wrap around her torso. His sweet breath kissing the back of her neck. With a cluck, Star breaks into a fast trot.

"Any idea where it could be coming from?" she asks.

"No. I'd imagine everyone would be out for this festival. I guess someone could have left a candle burning?"

May shrugs her shoulders. Star transitions to lope as they approach the main road. The smoke is thickening and expanding. The stars that were once as visible and bright as the moon are now muddied. Approaching the fork in the road, the smoke is heavier towards the direction of Clint's farm. An uneasy feeling bubbles in May's stomach. Clint's arms wrap tighter around her as Star's pace quickens. Slowly, the flames become visible, tearing through Clint's home and barn.

Star throws her hooves into the ground, jumping sideways and sending Clint into the dirt. Before May can ask if he's okay, he's already on his feet, running towards the barn.

"Clint what are you doing?"

He doesn't stop, he keeps running. May digs her heels into Star, but the young horse only rears. *Shit.* Clint is nowhere in sight. She slides out of the saddle and quickly ties the reins around a tree branch. May runs towards the barn. The doors are slid open. The wood is buckling under the fire.

"CLINT?"

Heart beating out of her chest, she doesn't know what to do. Her heart tells her to run into the barn, but her mind knows better. Suddenly, a silhouette appears in the doorway. The back of his shirt is burning as he leads out a limping Moon. Moon is burnt, badly, almost beyond recognition. Large patches of her grey hair are gone, with deep fleshy pink burns in their place. Her tail, which previously drug on the ground is singed and sticking out in different directions. The horse's front legs are bleeding, gashed and splintered by the broken wood. Her right eye is partially closed, blood seeps from the inner corner. Clint drags the horse to May, before taking his shirt off. He throws it to the ground and stomps the flames out.

Moon flinches as Clint strokes her neck. He pulls away, running his hands through his hair. Broken out in a cold sweat, his entire body is trembling. Moon's front legs crumble under her and she falls to her side. Her breaths are labored. Clint falls down beside her. He's crying. His shaky hand caresses her forehead.

"I don't k-know if I can do this," he looks up to May, "I'm n-not ready-y to lose her... We've been through so much, I wouldn't be here today, without her... I wouldn't have met you."

May kneels down next to him, a slow, steady stream of tears are cascading down her cheeks. She bites her lip. Moon is special to Clint, just as Red was to May, maybe even more so. For the longest time, all Clint had was Moon. He didn't know his parents or any of his family for that matter. While most looked at Moon as just a horse, she was more, she was family to him.

"Clint... she's suffering."

Clint swallows the lump in his throat. His expression is similar to a frightened child.

"I d-don't... I don't have my gun," he pulls out a hunting knife from his waistband, "t-this... is all I have."

There's no way either of them could make it to the house to retrieve one of his guns, and it would take too long to ride back to May's house, get her gun, and come back. May pulls her hand to her mouth, forcefully keeping the vomit inside her mouth. It burns all the way back down her throat.

Feebly grasping the knife's handle, he holds it above the horse's temple. *He can't do it... he shouldn't have to.* May pries the knife from his fingers. He pulls his hand away. She takes a deep breath. Clint lays his head against the horse's shoulder. With as much force as she can muster, she plunges the knife into the horse. It feels like everything is happening in slow motion, but immediately Moon stops breathing. Clint's sobbing worsens. May withdraws the knife and casts it away from them. Carefully, she puts her arm around his back and lays down next to him and Moon, while the flames crackle and pop in the background.

The morning sun is unwelcome as it crashes in through the bedroom window. May hadn't gotten any sleep that night. She had set up in the bed, staring at the dark walls. Clint is lying beside her. His back, suffering from a fourth-degree burn, is wrapped in linen. Silently, he had wept until he fell asleep.

May walks downstairs. She should be hungry, but the thought of food is repulsive. She can't get the image of Moon out of her mind. Puffy bags are under both her eyes, and her arms are peppered with dirt specks. On the kitchen counter, next to a full glass of water, lies a lock of Moon's tail. She had cut out a small section, untouched by the flames, for Clint. There's a soft knock at the door. May doesn't move. Aimlessly, she stares out the kitchen window. Star is in the pasture, peacefully grazing with the flock.

The door creaks open. "May?"

Felix walks into the kitchen. Dirt is smudged on his forehead and stained on his orange-colored pants.

"It took us a few hours to dig the hole, but she's buried." he says.

May continues to stare out the window.

"Greg came out with us. He searched the property. Found some smashed liquor bottles and quite a few matches... he thinks the fire was intentional," May turns and faces him, "but there's no clues on who started it."

"How long have you lived in Pine Valley?" she asks.

"All my life, same as you, why?"

"Do you remember it ever being like *this*?"

He shrugs his shoulders.

"Come on, Felix. This is the most uneventful place I can think of. We're so boring, we have festivals for literally everything, flowers, the fucking moon, EVERYTHING. Before this, the biggest thing to happen to this sleepy little town was John's suicide."

"I guess. What's your point?"

"My point is," she lowers her voice, "Pine Valley is no longer the place it used to be. I don't know what's changed."

"Well, Clint is here now."

"So, it's his fault?"

"No, uh, you know what I mean. He's the only thing that's new."

She shakes her head. "No."

"Then what?"

"I don't know, but I don't think I can live here any longer."

Felix's eyes widen.

"W-what are you saying?"

"I'm saying, I'm going to sell my flock, this house, and Clint and I are getting as far away from this place as we can."

"You... would leave?"

"Are you really this ignorant? Did you not see what happened? Someone burnt Clint's farm to the ground, injuring his horse to the point that I had to end her suffering. Everyone knew how much Moon meant to him," she runs her fingers through her tangled hair, "and that's not the first thing to happen. My sheep, my chickens, and now this... I don't think this is all some crazy coincidence."

"But Greg is here now, he's going to get the bottom of this!"

"Felix, I'm scared. I didn't think things could get worse, but they did. Even if Greg somehow managed to catch the person or persons responsible, the image of this town is tainted in my mind."

Felix grabs a seat at the table, crossing his arms in front of him.

"May, does this have anything to do with what I said to you?"

She shakes her head.

"No, Felix. I'll give it to you, you did surprise me, but no. Part of me thinks, maybe, in a different life, we could've ended up together, but I love Clint more than anything. I can't imagine waking up next to anyone else. God, I would do anything for him, and I know he would do the same for me."

Felix stands up. "All right."

He walks to her and pulls her into a hug. She wraps her arms around him.

"I will never stop caring about you, no matter where you go. And I can't promise you I won't cry when you leave, but I want you to be happy," a tear slips down his cheek, "no matter what that means."

Chapter 11

It's a cool autumn morning. Clint and May are standing at the back of her property, under a large pine tree. A few feet in front of the tree, the dirt is disturbed. A large rock, tan and smooth, sits atop the dirt. Beneath the rock and the dirt, is where Moon is buried.

It's been almost two weeks since Clint's farm was burned. Most of Clint's possessions were destroyed in the fire save two pistols, a shotgun, and some pots and pans. A large percentage of his herd had been injured and had to be shot. The handful of cows and calves he had left were sold to an out of town farmer. Brian had not asked about purchasing them, but even if he had, Clint would have still sold them to someone else.

"I guess a part of me will always be in Pine Valley," Clint says.

May reaches for his hand, their fingers interlace. She takes a deep breath.

"I've always wanted to leave this place and never look back. I still want to leave, but there are some fond memories I want to look back on: meeting you, the ball, how our relationship has formed."

Clint smiles. "No matter what, I want you to know, I don't regret moving here. Meeting you was the best thing that ever happened to me."

"I know."

May laughs. He gently nudges her shoulder.

"Are you sure you're ready to leave everything behind, Felix, your home, and move? I mean, I don't know where we're going to end up."

May nods. "I've never been more ready than I am now. I told Felix, and I think he understands. All that's left to do is talk to Mark about releasing my property."

"And you're doing that today?"

"Yes. The sooner the better."

She squeezes Clint's hand.

"Well maybe we could go into town together. I could check out that... what was it called, uh, Flower Festival? Isn't that today? I thought I heard Felix mention something."

"Oh right, I forgot, yeah, that's today. I do have a few things to take care of before I head into town, would you rather just head on? We could meet up after my meeting with Mark."

"Sure, as long as you don't keep me waiting too long."

She smiles. "I promise, I won't."

Together, they walk back towards her house, hand in hand. He pulls her into a tight embrace and kisses her, before he starts towards the road. May watches him walk out of eyesight before entering the house.

As part of the festival, townsfolk set up small garden displays using their best home-grown flowers. Displays feature a wide variety of flowers, from the orange and red hues of the helenium to the golden and yellow witch hazel. May has never been a participant of the festival before, but she would usually attend just to observe the exotic flowers.

May's chores ran longer than she intended, and it's been almost two hours since she last saw Clint. Her meeting with Mark has no particular scheduled time, but she had been hoping to get it over with before the crowds came into town. Unfortunately, it's too late, and the square is already packed with strangers and familiar faces alike.

Some are gawking at the flowers, some scolding their children for being fussy, and many catching up with old friends. The cool air is gone, replaced by a dry, humid heat. A few mosquitoes linger around from the night prior. To avoid the crowd, May decides to walk in the alley behind the buildings. The different pollen scents are strong but not strong enough to overtake the crowd's sweaty stench. She walks behind the butcher and towards the bank when something catches her eye.

The pavement, ten feet ahead of her, seems to be stained. May hustles forward, pausing at the red blotches that lie before her. She bends down, running her pale finger against the colored stone. *Blood? I thought the town had been scrubbed spotless for today.* She shakes her head, slightly relieved the town was not able to complete the farce of perfection, and instead catches a glimmer of something strange. May's head slowly cranes left, towards the compost pile. The hairs on the back of her neck stand up and a ghostly shiver summons chill bumps on her arms and legs. A mass is sitting against the heap. She rises and shuffles slowly towards the mangled mess. As she gets closer, she sees him.

There, right in front of her very eyes, lies Clint. Her Clint, or the shell of the body that used to be him. May lets out a blood curdling scream and falls to her knees. Hot tears flush out of her eyes as she begins crawling over to his lifeless body.

"Please, no... Clint, oh please..." May whispers.

Her hands shake uncontrollably as she reaches out to touch Clint's cold, limp arm. His icy flesh cripples her heartbeat. He's barely recognizable, lying in a pool of his own blood. Clint's eyes are as glassy as a lake frozen during the winter. His hair is tinted putridly with blood crusted on his curls. Clint's bare chest is no longer smooth, instead it's riddled with gashes. May caresses his cheek, her fingers refusing to meet the slash under his eye. She feels the presence of a crowd drawing around her as her head begins to throb. Her eyelids flutter as her vision begins to blur. May embraces him, holding her entire world in her arms, shortly before she loses consciousness and falls limp.

It's eleven o'clock in the morning. The sky is grey. Occasionally the clouds open up, releasing patchy drizzles onto the dry earth. May stands at the far corner of her pasture. Puffy bags are under both her bloodshot eyes. A dress, simple and black, hangs on her body. A few feet from where she stands, underneath a massive pine tree, the tallest one in the pasture, is a hole. The hole, around eight feet long and four feet wide, is destined to be Clint's final resting place.

May doesn't know what day of the week it is. Ever since she found him, like *that*, all her days have run together. Every time she closes her eyes, she sees his body. Every time the image flashes in her mind, it chips away a small piece of her. It won't be long before there is nothing left of her, just her body, an empty shell surrounded by darkness.

The jingling of harnesses echoes through the pines as a horse-drawn wagon approaches the property. The wagon, pulled by two muscular Belgian draft horses, carries a pine box. The box, seven feet long, three feet wide, and three and half feet deep, houses Clint's body. Guiding the wagon is a gentleman by the name of Morris. He's the closest person to be considered a doctor. Besides knowing how to make ointments and remedies for basic colds and stitching up a few gashes here and there, he has never had any formal training on the practice of medicine. He only learned by watching his father, who had gotten professional training up in a northern, overpopulated town. His brown skin is thin and riddled with wrinkles. His hair is white, and thin.

"May?"

She turns. Felix is standing behind her. He's dressed in dark brown cotton britches and a black shirt. His expression holds a level of grief. Not for the loss of Clint, but for the mourning of May.

"We've gotten just about everything set up inside, Morris and a few guys are bringing in the body," he stops himself,

"Clint. They're bringing in Clint. The service is going to start soon."

May nods. A lone tear slips down her cheek. Felix offers his arm to her. Shakily, she takes it. Her stomach is empty, but the overwhelming urge to vomit is pressing against her throat. They're not walking towards the house, they're walking to say goodbye to Clint. It's the end of it all. Never again will she see his face, feel his skin against hers, breathe his sweet kisses, hear his laugh. This is it.

The casket is positioned in against the far wall in the living room. The furniture is rearranged in rows. Not expecting to draw a crowd, the only additional seating is by the kitchen chairs. Flowers, ironically from the festival, are displayed in no particular theme. Roses red and white, lay at the base of the box. Yellow carnations are on top the table, orange lilies are scattered on the ground.

The attendance is small, as expected. Royce and Mark are chatting quietly by the casket. Nina is sitting in a chair next to Becca. Both girls are attired in all black. It seems that, for once, Becca doesn't have an agenda. Morris is standing in the back, next to the sheriff. Felix leads May to the front of the room.

"Shall we begin?" Mark asks.

May nods. Felix helps her to the couch. He takes a seat beside her, his hand still holding hers. Royce sits down in a chair next to Nina.

Mark clears his throat. "Thank you all for coming. Today, we are gathered here to celebrate Clint's life and to say our goodbyes. While Clint was only in Pine Valley for several months, his presence will be sorely missed. At this time, I would like to invite Ms. Ferrothorn up to say a few words. After all she knows... knew, him best."

May looks fragile, like a flower on the verge of wilting. She can't help but think about that day. She told him not to wait on her, encouraged him to go. What if he had stayed? Or maybe, it was because she took so long with her chores. Either way she looks at it, he died because she was not there with him. Maybe, her presence wouldn't have stopped his death, maybe it would have resulted in her being murdered too; however, at least in that scenario, they would still be together.

"Do you want me go up there with you?" Felix asks.

She shakes her head, taking her hand from his. Her hand caresses the side of the casket as she walks up. Mark gently touches her shoulder, as if it would offer any comfort, before retreating to a seat next to his daughter.

May takes a deep breath. She imagines Clint standing beside her, his hand resting on her back. If only he were there, if only she could touch him one last time, if only she could see that crooked grin spread across his face. A tear slips down her cheek.

"I think I met Clint by pure luck... I'm not sure if it was good luck or bad luck, considering why we're here. Before I met him, I was stuck in an old, never-ending routine. Each day beginning and ending the same as the day prior. He taught me how to live, how to *really* live. He gave me purpose, joy, and love. Not the kind of love that husbands and wives claim to have, not the love that a boy has for his mother, not even that which is claimed to be between young lovers. It was real, passionate, and unbridled. He saw my flaws, but thought I was flawless. He saw my scars, but thought I was beautiful. He saw the worst of me, but loved me anyway. I used to think there was someone out there, godly or otherwise, that made the universe the way it is. I know now, this is not true. Nothing, not even a divine being, would be cruel enough to bring Clint in my life, make me fall in love, and then take him away. So please, keep your prayers to yourself. I'm not looking for your spiritual guidance and I'm sure as hell not looking for your pity. The only thing that may help me sleep again at night will be finding the monster who did this," her eyes lock with Greg's, "and killing them."

Suddenly the window shatters as a rock flies into the room. Becca squeals, cowering behind the kitchen chair. Nina crouches down next to her. Shortly after, another rock crashes into the room. Defensively, Felix jumps in front of May. Greg rushes to the door and opens it. Standing in the tall grass, all by himself, is Brian. A large whiskey bottle is in his left hand, another fist-sized rock in his right.

"Am I late?" he asks

"Stop this right now," Greg yells.

Brian throws the third rock towards the sheriff, barely missing his knee. Royce and Mark exchange worried glances.

"I didn't want tah miss this," he takes a drink of the bottle, "… damn, it's empty."

"Mr. Grey, don't make me tell you again."

Brian furrows his brow. He pulls his arm back and throws the bottle as hard as he can. It smashes through the window and shatters on the ground. Becca screams again and someone shushes her. May pushes past Felix. He grabs her arm but she shakes him off, making her way to the door. There's an intense heat burning in the back of her head.

"Do you have something you want to say?" she asks.

"Do not engage," Greg starts, but May puts her hand up, silencing him.

Brian straightens his stance, puffing out his chest. "You bet I do."

"Then say it," she steps out on the front porch, extending her arms, "we're all listening."

"He got what he deserved. That bastard spread lies about me and killed my ma."

The heat in the back of May's head intensifies. Tears are welling in her eyes. She balls her hands into fists.

"Did you do this?" her voice is barely above a whisper.

Brian takes a step back, a chuckle escapes his fat lips.

"No, but I wish to God I had."

His words are the final straw. In one swift motion, May pulls the pistol from Greg's holder. Two clicks. One hits his stomach, the other just below the belt. He falls without a sound. If anyone screamed, May didn't hear it. She drops the gun as she feels hands on her shoulders, Felix's. He spins her around. His eyes are panic-stricken.

"What did you just do?" he asks.

Tears stream down May's cheeks. She throws herself into Felix, burying her face in his chest. Greg and Royce run to Brian. Blood is pooling in his gaped mouth. The two men look at each other. They don't have to check for a pulse, he's gone.

"I had nothing left, nothing to lose. The day he died, I died too."

"You have me, May. You've *always* had me."

Greg walks up to May. He runs his hands through his hair and takes a deep breath. All eyes are locked on him.

"I told you not to engage."

May wakes up. She's lying on the couch, Felix is sitting on the ground, holding her hand. Her head is pounding, and her body is covered in a cold sweat.

"Felix?" she says.

He looks at her, a weak smile on his face. "Hey."

"What happened?"

She sits up. The room is spinning. Flowers are still on the floor, but the casket is gone. All the furniture is back to its original place. It's quiet and the sun is no longer shining. *Was I dreaming?*

"Brian showed up after you gave your eulogy. He was super drunk, yelling some nonsense about his mother and threatening to come beat up Clint. Greg and Mark had to go out and apprehend him. I turned my back for just a few seconds, and I heard a thud. You were on the ground."

"Oh," she rubs her temples, "how long was I out?"

"A few hours."

"That long? W-where's Clint?"

Felix sighs. "We took care of him."

"You mean h-he's already gone... buried? Why didn't you wait, or wake me up?"

"May... you haven't slept in days... I just, couldn't."

"I just wanted to see him," she chokes back tears, "one last time."

He shakes his head. "You didn't need to see him like that."

May stands up abruptly, her legs almost failing her. Felix acts like he's ready to catch her. He puts his hands on her arms, but she pushes him away.

"Don't touch me! You had no right to make that decision for me!"

"May, I was just trying to help..."

She shoves him harder, knocking him back. "I don't need your help. I don't want *anything* from you."

"Please don't say that."

She can no longer contain her tears. They flow down her cheeks with ease. Felix reaches his hand out and she slaps it away.

"Get out, just go!"

His eyes are pained. He opens his mouth to protest, but nothing comes out. Dejectedly, he walks to the door. His hand rests on the doorknob.

"If you need anything," he opens the door, "you know where to find me."

She waits a few minutes, afraid he might still be outside the door, but when she opens it, he isn't. There's no one there, only the moon and her livestock to keep her company. Slowly she walks to the pasture, not because of the low visibility, but because she's physically exhausted. The few hours she was out did nothing to alleviate her weakened state. Her flock had already investigated the fresh dirt mound, many of the flowers had been nibbled, few had any petals at all. May lies down on the cold dirt. *Nothing. I can't feel him.* Tears well up in her eyes. She brushes some of the dirt onto her skin. *Why couldn't they have taken me too?*

12

Chapter 12

"Greg took him back to Oak Ridge," Felix taps May on the shoulder, "hey are you even listening to me?"

May looks up from her untouched plate of pancakes. Her fork has twirled circles in the cake, mutilating its shape. She nods. It's been almost three weeks since the funeral. May is still in a state of shock. Every morning she turns to the right side of the bed, his side, expecting to see him lying next to her. Every morning her heart sinks as the realization that he's gone settles in. During the day, she looks outside, as if he's going to be out in the pasture, brushing Star or napping against a tree. He never is. When she returns the evening, she just *knows* he's going to be in the house cooking dinner or waiting to scoop her into his arms and carry her to the bedroom. Every time he's not there, it gets more real. He's never coming back.

"What did I say?"

She averts his gaze. "I'm sorry, I just zoned out a bit."

"What I said was, Greg took Brian back to Oak Ridge. After investigating Jason's old property, he said there was enough evidence to link Brian to the crime. Something about the bullets matching up to some they found in the slaughterhouse. They still haven't found the gun that fired them, though."

May looks back down at her breakfast. "I see."

"They've put up some temporary fencing around the house. I think they're still looking," he lowers his voice, "they think he might have something to do with..."

"You know, you can say it. I'm not as fragile as you think."

"I'm sorry," he lightly lays his hand above hers, "after his behavior at the funeral, it's hard not to think he was involved in Clint's death, someway, somehow."

May's stomach churns. Her throat burns. *Not again.* She runs to the front door, barely making it to the edge of the porch. She doesn't throw up much, considering how little she's eaten the past few days, but it still stings.

"Hey, are you okay?" Felix asks.

May turns to him. She places a hand on her cramping stomach. Her skin is two shades paler than it normally is.

"Yes," she takes his extended hand, "I've just haven't been feeling myself lately."

Felix escorts her back into her house and onto the couch. She lies down, laying her arm over her eyes. It feels like the entire room is spinning, even the couch. The windows still haven't been repaired, only a few boards had been nailed up as a temporary barrier to keep any unwanted creatures from entering the house.

"How long has this been going on?"

"I don't know, a few weeks, maybe?"

"May, you have got to take care of yourself. I know what you're going," he quickly stops himself, "What I *meant* to say is Clint wouldn't want to see you like this. You're never hungry when I come over, I haven't seen you in town in over a week, it's like you've shut yourself off from the world."

"Maybe it's your cooking."

He rolls his eyes. "Be serious please."

"Fine," she sits up, "if it's really worrying you so much, I'll take Star out on a ride this afternoon. Would that make you happy?"

"By yourself? Are you sure that's a good idea?"

"Yes, by myself. Would you rather I just stay inside?"

He bites his lip. "No."

It's an unusually warm fall afternoon. The air is stale and the wind is nonexistent. Sweat is lathered on Star's neck. The heat doesn't curb her energy, she's chomping at the bit and swishing her tail as she trots. May is sweating herself, layered in a dark-colored sleeveless shirt with a beige button-up shirt on top.

She pats Star's neck. "Easy girl."

Riding was something she always used as an escape, to get out of her head and away from her problems. Now, it hurts. Maybe it's because Clint gave her Star or maybe it's because all the time they spent riding together, whatever the case, it just makes her miss him more. Something she didn't realize was even plausible.

"Whoa," she reigns Star to a stop.

As Felix said, a makeshift fence is surrounding the front of Brian's house. Posts, hastily pushed into the dry soil, are tethered together with rusted barbwire. A wooden square sign marked "DO NOT ENTER" in red paint, is nailed to one of the posts. May dismounts Star and walks to the fence. Her fingers grab a post. It wobbles under her touch. She pushes harder and it falls back, pulling down wire with it. She carefully leads Star over the fallen wire, and towards the back of the property. May ties the horse to Brian's wagon which is parked behind the house.

"I'll be right back," she says.

She walks back to the front of the house. The doorknob jiggles but doesn't budge. She looks over her shoulder. *No one*. She takes off her button-up shirt and wraps it around her hand, making a fist. The glass breaks easily. She reaches her hand through the shattered remnants and unlocks the door.

The interior of the home is quaint, but messy. Broken glass bottles are littered across the dark stained floors. The walls, painted a soft lilac, are blemished by holes about the size of a fist. Probably Brian's doing. The furniture is old, snags run up and down the tartan chairs. On an end table sits a basket of yarn and an unfinished crocheted item, maybe a scarf or hat, clearly untouched after Annabelle's death.

May maneuvers into the kitchen. There are dirty dishes on the counter, and a broken glass on the floor. Some cockroaches are feasting on a molded cake. She pulls open the drawers one by one, looking for anything that might resemble the knife that was left at her property. The silverware set is old, clearly used, but none hold that wooden handle. She searches the cupboards to no avail. *Maybe it was old, part of a different set, but where would it be besides the kitchen?*

She walks through the living area to the first bedroom, it's the master. A full-sized bed sits in the corner. There's a pink quilt covering it. *Annabelle's room.* A large mirror sits on a dresser, pressed against the far wall. It's coated in a thin layer of dust. On the top of the dresser lies a hairbrush with a wooden handle. She opens the drawers, which are filled with clothes, and pats the clothes, checking for any abnormalities, but doesn't dig them out. Regardless of Brian's cruelty, Annabelle was nothing but kind. There's no way she would've had anything to do with that happened, she wouldn't have condoned it.

The second bedroom, Brian's, is messy. Clothes are thrown all over the floor. The bed is unmade, a dark blue quilt hangs off the corner. There's a bookshelf with several older books that are so old that their titles are illegible, along with a few knick-knacks. A sweaty odor hangs in the air, as if the room was slept in only the day prior. May kicks around some of the clothes, but only trash is uncovered. *If I were trying to hide something, where would be the best spot?* Her eyes fall to the bed. Begrudgingly, she gets on her hands and knees. She reaches under the bed, blindly clawing until her hand grasps a thin leather-bound book.

May sits up and holds the book in her hands. Upon closer inspection, it's not a book, it's a journal. The journal itself is old, there's dark splotches on the leather. On the interior cover there's a note in dainty handwriting, "For my dearest Brian, love Mama". The next pages are sloppy, stained, with messy scribbles. May strains to read the notes, it looks like a list of some sort.

"~~Mary~~

~~Bella~~

Matthew

Josh

~~Jason~~

Sam

Rebecca"

May raises her eyebrow. *Jason and Rebecca? Like his former business partner, Jason? And does this stand for Becca?* She flips the page. There's a short paragraph.

"Today was progress. Mary's mother finally left her alone in the shop. I tried talking with her, and this time, she didn't run away. I gave her a daisy from Mama's vase and she smiled at me. I asked her if she would come back again soon and she said she would be back Friday."

She flips to the next page. There's a poor drawing resembling a girl holding a flower. There's smudges and random ink marks, where he scribbled over parts of the drawing instead of just starting over. There's another paragraph on the back.

"Friday came and went, Mary never showed up. Mama says not to worry, she probably got busy, but I know better. She's just like the rest of them. Next time I see her, I'll teach her a lesson. I'll show her what it feels like to be alone, really alone."

Underneath is a depiction of a girl crying, covered in spiders and other crawlers. *What did you do to her?* Suddenly, there's a pain as May is struck in the back of the head, rendering her unconscious.

May regains consciousness on Felix's bed. A thin blanket covers her body. There's an intense throbbing in the back of her head. She sits up and the throbbing intensifies.

"Are you okay?" Felix asks.

May jumps. He is sitting on a chair in the corner of the room, a sketchpad is in his lap.

"Shit, I didn't see you there," she says.

He laughs light-heartedly. "Sorry, didn't mean to scare you."

May rubs the back of her head. Light is coming from the window.

"Why am I here? What happened? What time is it?"

"Hey, slow down there. You're here because my dad found you unconscious on the side of the main road. You probably got bucked off or something, I don't really know," he looks out the window, "it's almost six, you've been here for a little over an hour."

"What? W-where's Star?"

"Don't worry, she's fine. He found her grazing in a field few yards from where you were."

"That's… impossible."

Felix cocks his head to the side. "What do you mean?"

"I was in," she hesitates, looking down at her hands, "I was in Brian's house."

"YOU WHAT?"

"Easy, I've got a headache…"

"What are you talking about? I already told you his house is fenced off."

May shrugs her shoulders. "It wasn't a very sturdy fence."

Felix rises to his feet, throwing his hands in the air. The sketchpad drops to the ground with a soft thud.

"Seriously, it's not that big of a deal."

"May, Brian is in the center of *two* different murder investigations going on right now. Going through his property could jeopardize the investigation."

"Or help. Who's to say they would've found anything?"

"Who's to say YOU would've?"

"But I did..."

Felix's eyes widen. "What did you find?"

"Some sort of journal. It had a list of names and weird writings... it was like he was keeping track of interactions with different people. The one I was reading was about some girl, he wrote he was going to punish her or something for standing him up."

"What else did it say?"

"... I don't know. Everything else after that is a blank. I was just reading and then, nothing."

Felix scratches the back of his head. "Maybe that fall took some of your memories?"

She squeezes her eyes shut. She can see the journal in her hand, she can smell the sweaty room, but then it goes dark. Nothing, just blackness.

"Did Royce say he found anything on me?"

Felix shakes his head. "If he found anything, he didn't mention it. I think he should be home in a few hours, you're more than welcome to stay for dinner and you could ask him then."

"I honestly just want to go home."

"Want me to walk with you?"

"No, I want to be alone."

Outside the tailor shop, Star is tied up. Her coat is curled from sweat. She impatiently paws at the gravel. May slides her hand under Star's fluffy forelock. Without another parting word, May steps in the saddle and rides away from the shop. The evening air is slightly cooler than what the afternoon was, but it's still hot. May can feel eyes on her as she rides through the town. She can hear the whispers through the pines. It was one thing, being judged for her relationship with Clint, but now, she's looked at differently. It's an entirely new reputation that she holds. She's the girl whose fiancé was murdered.

Chapter 13

There's a soft knock at May's door. It's Greg tailed by another man. He's a stranger not native to Pine Valley. The man appears older, maybe in his fifties. He's holding something wrapped up in an old blanket.

"Can we come in?" Greg asks.

"Please."

They follow her into the kitchen. The window is cracked, letting the morning air seep in. A plate of eggs, partially eaten, sits in the sink.

"Do you guys want something to drink?" she asks.

"No," they say in unison.

May takes a seat at the table. The stranger sets down the blanket.

"This is Chase, he works with me back in Oak Ridge," Greg gestures to the man, "he's been helping with the investigation into Clint's murder and the case against Brian."

"The reason we're here is that we found some evidence during our search. Do you still have the knife?" Chase asks.

May nods. She retrieves the knife from a kitchen drawer before returning to the table. The two men exchange glances. Carefully, Chase unfolds the blanket, revealing three forks, two spoons and a knife, all with wooden handles. He picks up May's knife and sets it next to the others. A set. The only difference between the knife used to slaughter her chickens and the one they found, is the stained blood tint on the blade. May feels lightheaded. She swallows a lump in her throat.

"W-where did you find these?"

"We did a full sweep of Brian's property, starting with the slaughterhouse and then the home. These were hiding in plain sight, in one of the kitchen drawers," Greg says.

In the kitchen drawer? May is speechless. She opens her mouth to speak but nothing comes out. It's suddenly hard to breathe, like the walls are closing in on her.

"Trust me," Greg picks up one of the forks, "we were just as surprised as you are. With this, we have enough to convict him of Clint's murder. Honestly, we might be able to forgo a trial completely. I think once we present the evidence to Mr. Grey, he will have no choice but to admit his guilt."

His words aren't penetrating her thoughts. All she sees are the drawers. The same drawers she saw with her own eyes, absent of the silverware. *Please stop.* May raises her trembling hand in the air.

"Ms Ferrothorn, are you all right? You're looking a little pale."

"Those... weren't there initially," she says. Her voice is barely above a whisper.

"I beg your pardon?"

"I was... I was there, last week. I searched through the house, starting with the kitchen," she shakes her head feverishly, "those were not there. I would've found them. I didn't find anything, except an old journal..."

Chase's eyes widen. "Wait just a minute. What do you mean you were *there*?"

"I just happened to be riding my horse by and noticed the door was open..."

"Are you kidding me," Greg slams his hand on the table, "Do you know what that means?"

May shakes her head.

"You being there puts the entire case in jeopardy. That is something that will have to be disclosed if we go to trial, honestly it would be enough to let him walk. The fact that you were inside his home could raise question as if you planted the evidence."

May throws her hands in the air. "THAT'S MY POINT. Obviously, I didn't plant it there, but it wasn't there when I initially went, so *someone* had to have been there besides me."

"What all do you remember when you were there?"

"I searched the kitchen, Annabelle's room, and then Brian's room where I found some journal under his bed. I was reading it and then... I don't know. I woke up at Felix's house."

Chase puts his hand up. "What do you mean *you don't know*?"

May shrugs her shoulders. "The last thing I remember was just being there, reading the journal. Next thing I knew, I was in Felix's bed."

The two men exchange a glance. May sighs.

"It wasn't like *that*."

Greg shakes his head. "That's not what I'm implying. How did you get from the house to Felix's?"

"I don't know. He said Royce found me on the side of the main road and my horse was grazing in some field."

Greg pulls out a writing pad and begins scribbling. "Correct me if I'm wrong, you are saying that last week, you went to Brian's property. You searched the house and didn't find the silverware; however, you found a journal. You were reading said journal and then all of the sudden you woke up at Felix's house?"

May nods. "Did you guys find the journal? It was leather-bound."

Greg flips back a few pages in the notebook. He scans a list of scribbles. Chase leans over, eyeing the list.

"Yes. We did find a journal; however, it was not in Brian's bedroom."

"Where was it?"

"The living room area."

Someone had to have moved it... or did I? She closes her eyes, again, trying to remember the events that led her to waking up at Felix's, but it's no use. Nothing.

"So, what's the next step?" she asks.

"In light of this development, we're going to need to talk with Royce," Greg rocks back in his chair, "I will have to disclose with my colleagues that you were on the property. If I'm being brutally honest, that could be a breaking point in this case. Regardless, Brian is still being kept at the station while we investigate the possible murder of his neighbor... you didn't happen to go to that property as well, did you?"

"No sir."

"Good," Greg sits forward and places his hands on the table. "At this point, this is still an open investigation. I will give you a verbal warning for trespassing on Mr. Grey's property, but if it happens again, I will have to take legal actions. Understood?"

May nods. "I understand."

Greg picks up the original knife. "Can we take this?"

"Yes," May takes a deep breath, "But can you promise me something?"

Greg nods.

"Please... don't get tunnel vision. I know Brian is guilty, but I don't know what he's guilty of. He blamed Clint for Annabelle's death and he's made himself an easy suspect, but I think other people know this too."

The first day of winter is cold. A light layer of snow covers the ground. It's not the type of snow that crunches and breaks as you step on it; instead, it's the type of snow that's soft and sticks to every surface it encounters. The windows of May's house are cloudy. A few flakes are stuck on the outside paneling.

May is standing in front of her mirror, studying her appearance. Her pants are snugger than they used to be. Her fingers pinch at the stomach fat. Nina sits on May's bed. She has a thin blanket draped over her shoulders. Her eyes are locked on May.

"I mean you guys were having sex... right?" Nina asks.

"Y-yes, but I don't think that has anything to with this."

"When was the last time you had your period?"

May rocks back on her heels. "Maybe... Two months? No, that can't, be right..."

"I don't want to scare you, but you have to look at the facts. You've put on a little weight, you've been feeling nauseous on almost a daily basis, and you haven't bled in two months," Nina takes a deep breath. "Honestly, May I think you're pregnant."

May's stomach drops to her knees. *Pregnant? No...* She fights the urge to cry. It's one thing to be alone, but it's another to be alone with a child. She pictures Clint, standing in front of her, his eyes welling up with tears and a smile spreading across his entire face at the news of her pregnancy. He would've been happy.

"Have you talked to Felix about this?" Nina asks.

May shakes her head. She walks to the bed and sits down next to Nina.

"Honestly," May lays her head on Nina's shoulder, "I wouldn't know where to even begin. We haven't been seeing each other as much lately, I'm not sure what's going on."

"Busy season?"

"I guess. There's just a lot of things going on with the investigation and everything. I have so much going through my head, sometimes I feel like I don't know who I can trust."

"Have you regained any memories or anything from when you were in Brian's house?"

"No, and the more I think about it, the more it concerns me."

"What do you mean?"

"I was in Brian's house and then I wasn't," May fidgets with her fingers, "I don't remember going back outside, getting on Star, or riding away. You'd at least think I would remember *that*."

"You said you woke up Felix's, right?"

May nods. "It's like... he's always there when I *need* him. I hate myself for thinking this but..."

"But what?"

"What if Royce didn't find me? What if Felix did? I don't mean found me in the road, I mean found me in the house. What if he found me, panicked or something, and hit me?"

"Are you suggesting that he had something to do with Clint's murder?"

"I don't know. How did Greg find that silverware after I searched the kitchen? I don't think this is all one big coincidence," May sighs, "Felix asked me, 'What if I told you I loved you', and then it was this downward spiral in my life with Clint's farm burning down, and his murder."

Nina takes a deep breath but doesn't say anything. May falls back onto the bed, crossing her arms. It's silent, save for the wind brushing against the side of the house.

"You know," Nina shifts her body to look at May, "we haven't really talked about Clint in quite some time. Are you doing okay?"

May closes her eyes. "No."

She can picture him, smiling. Sometimes she can still feel his presence, when she's lying alone in bed or out riding Star. His clothes are starting to lose his scent, which hurts, but they still bring comfort. She finds herself wearing his shirts when no one is around, crying quietly, and cursing the world for taking him from her. He was the one light in her life, now it's dark.

"I know we don't get to see each other as often as we'd both like, but please remember that no matter what, I'm always here for you, May. Even if you just need someone to vent to, or sit by you and say nothing, you can come to me."

His image muddies in her mind. Now it's Felix with his back turned to her. He's holding something, a large knife. Clint is in front of him, holding his hands up defensively. They're talking, but she can't hear anything. Suddenly Felix lunges forward and his knife makes contact with Clint, slashing through his skin like paper. May opens her eyes. A lone tear slides down her cheek. *Could Felix really do that? He knew what Clint meant to me...*

There's a harsh knock at the door.

"Are you expecting anyone?" Nina asks.

May shakes her head. She pulls herself from the bed and slowly shuffles downstairs. There's another knock, but it's softer.

"May, are you home?" Felix asks from the other side of the door.

"Yeah, come in," she says.

He opens the door carefully, as if trying to protect her home from the winter air. He's wearing a thick crimson overcoat lined with rabbit fur. He's holding a box under his left arm.

May forces a smile. "Hey."

"Hey."

Nina walks down the stairs. "Hi Felix."

He smiles at her.

"May, I'm going to go ahead and take off," she embraces May, "Remember, if you need anything, anything at all, come find me. It was nice seeing you Felix."

"You too Nina."

She leaves without another word. May follows Felix to the couch and they take a seat. He rests the box on his lap. It's wrapped in solid brown paper and tied with a thin yellow ribbon that's fashioned into a bow.

"How've you been? It's been a while," she says.

"Good, and I know, I'm sorry. Business at the shop has been good, a lot of people wanting coats. I have also been working on this," he looks down at the box. "It's actually for you."

"You didn't have to make me anything."

He hands her the box. "Just open it."

She releases the string bow and gently raises the lid. Her heart skips a beat, stealing the air from inside her body. It's a framed portrait of Clint. A sketch so lifelike and detailed, it's like a photograph. She can't hold in the tears, they glide off her face and onto the glass.

"Felix... you d-did this?"

"Yes. Honestly, I've been working on it since before the funeral. I was hoping to get it to you sooner, but I had to get it just *right*."

"It's perfect," she pulls the picture to her chest, "Thank you, this means the world to me."

"Anything for you."

May sets the picture back into the box and places it on the table. Felix extends his hand to hers and she takes it.

"Is everything okay with you? Things seemed a little... tense when I walked in."

She nods. "It's as okay as it can be... Nina thinks I'm pregnant."

Felix's mouth falls open. "WHAT?"

"I don't know. I've been feeling pretty nauseous lately," she looks down at her stomach, "and I've gained a little weight."

"A-are you sure it's not stress-related?"

"I... haven't had my period in two months either."

Felix shifts uncomfortably on the couch. "Oh."

"Yeah."

"What... what are you going to do?"

"I don't know, I'm a little scared. I barely take care of myself, how am I supposed to take care of a baby too?"

"Don't be scared," Felix pulls her into him and wraps his arms around her, "You're not alone in this."

Suddenly, the image of Felix stabbing Clint flashes in her mind. She pushes him away, recoiling to the other end of the couch.

"What's wrong?"

May shakes her head. "N-nothing."

Felix reaches his hand out to her, but she refuses it.

"Seriously, what's wrong?"

"Nothing really, I'm just on edge with everything. I feel like the investigation is at a standstill, it's been weeks and not a single word."

Felix shifts uncomfortably on the couch. "There's actually been some news."

"What?"

"It's not regarding to Clint's murder, no news on that; However, he has been formally charged with Jason's murder. Said there was some weird entries in a few journals. Also found a gun that held some bullets that matched the shell casings."

"I wonder if any of those journals mention Clint?"

Felix shrugs his shoulders. "They seem more hush hush about that part of the investigation. Although, they did some heavy questioning of my dad."

"That's strange," May forces a perplexed expression on her face. "Did they say why?"

"Not really, they were mainly asking questions about *you*. Honestly, it seemed like you were a suspect."

Her mouth falls open. "Are you serious?"

"I wouldn't worry about it too much. I mean, you did go into Brian's house," Felix stands up. "I have to get going, but I did have a question for you."

"What is it?"

"Do... do you have any plans for the holidays?"

May shakes her head.

"Well, would you be willing to be my plus one to the Christmas banquet?"

"I don't know Felix. I don't really feel like celebrating Christmas this year."

"Come on May, it would be good to get out. Besides, you were missed at Thanksgiving."

"Have you seen the way everyone looks at me now? It's a weird combination of pity and curiosity. I think facing that firsthand sounds like a terrible idea."

"You wouldn't be alone. I promise, I would stay by your side the entire night, and if things get hairy, we could just leave."

May sighs. "I will consider going, but don't get your hopes up."

14

Chapter 14

Christmas Eve morning brought a thick and heavy snow, as well as doubts and feelings of anxiety. By evening time, the snow is still in its same state, but the feelings of anxiety have tripled. May sits on her bed, staring at her hands. The portrait of Clint is now hanging on an open space in the wall, next to the window. She's wearing brown cotton pants and a solid red shirt, probably too casual for the banquet, which she still isn't sure that she's even going to.

She grabs he sheepskin coat and forces herself to go downstairs. Before she's hit the last step, the front door blows open. It's Felix. He's fashioned in red britches, a white shirt, and his rabbit fur-lined coat.

"Merry Christmas Eve," he says.

"Hi Felix."

"Where's your Christmas spirit? And are you going like that or are you going to change first?"

May rolls her eyes. "I don't have any. *If* I go, I'm not changing."

"Fair enough. I did get a carriage."

"Always over the top?"

Felix grins. "Of course."

The Christmas banquet is always held at the Miller's luxurious house. The home is spacious with four bedrooms, a large library and grand dining hall. Even with all the space, the venue can feel overcrowded with the extensive guest list. Everyone in town is invited and Mark also invites some out of town family members as well.

May and Felix are the last guests to arrive. A stranger at the door takes their coats. Voices are echoing throughout the halls. A large fir tree, strung up with ribbons, wooden ornaments and a popcorn garland, sits in the middle of the room. Becca stands beside the tree, wearing a tight red dress, sipping some ale from a glass cup. She's too busy talking to a blonde stranger, wearing an equally tight black dress, to notice Felix and May walk in.

Felix throws his arm around May. "Quickly please."

He drags May into the dining room. The rectangular table is set for twenty guests with large silver plates, sparkling clean silverware, and red and green place mats. A few guests have already taken their seats, but the majority are standing around talking.

"Felix! May! I'm so happy you guys are here," Nina says.

She rushes to the friends, gifting them both with a hug. She's dressed in a plain white dress and scuffed shoes. Her cheeks are full and flushed. Felix steps away and goes to his father, who appears to be having an intense conversation with Mark.

"I didn't think you were coming?"

"I didn't think I was either," May looks at Felix. "He asked me to come."

"Does this mean you've abandoned your suspicions?"

May shakes her head. "I have this weird gut feeling, but part of me is mad at myself for even considering him as a suspect."

Mark clanks the side of a wine glass with a spoon. "Everyone, it's almost seven. If you could please take a seat at the table, dinner will be served soon."

The chatter muffles momentarily while chairs are claimed. Mark at the head of the table, beside him are Becca and the blonde she was speaking with earlier. Royce takes the opposite end of the table, next to Felix. May sits in between Felix and Nina. Morris sits opposite to Nina. All other chairs are taken by strangers, minus one.

Wine as red as blood is poured into every glass, but water is not offered. A large bowl of salad, baked ham, seasoned potatoes and fresh green beans are strategically placed on the table. It's the family-style kind of dinner where you take your portion and pass the bowl onto the next. Maybe it's just her nerves but May feels the eyes of the room on her. It's nauseating. She takes little of each item, her plate less than halfway full.

"Are you okay?" Felix asks.

She nods.

"I would like to thank everyone who came out tonight to spend Christmas Eve with my lovely daughter and me. I hope you know that I consider you all a part of my family, regardless of blood or ties," Mark raises his glass. "With that being said, please enjoy your meal."

The room erupts with joyous laughter and conversation. May pokes at her food with a fork. The ham is dry. She looks to the empty seat. *Who is that for?* Christmas Eve would've been different with Clint. They wouldn't have come to this silly dinner, they probably wouldn't have even still been in this town. Cooking dinner and sitting around a table all to themselves. She can still hear his laughter.

"Have you already moved on May?" Becca asks, her voice as shrill as ever.

May looks up from her plate. "What?"

"I just think it's an *interesting* coincidence seeing you here with Felix. Clint's been gone for what, maybe two months?"

Silence. Mouths are gaping. All eyes are on a speechless May. The room is suddenly constricting. May's heart rate increases. She opens her mouth to speak, but nothing comes out.

Felix slams his fist on the table. "Becca shut up."

"Why? I'm just saying what's on everyone else's minds," she takes a sip of her drink, "I guess this could be a ploy just to get out of having a bastard."

May, with tears in her eyes, looks to Felix. "Y-you told her?"

"I guess the rumors are true..."

"Seriously Becca shut up," Felix turns to May. "No, I would never have told her. You know how I feel about her."

He reaches for May's hand, but she yanks it away.

"Who else would've told her Felix?"

Tears are building in her eyes. She pushes herself from the table, and trots to the door. Felix is hot on her heels.

"May wait, please," he grabs her shoulder. "Slow down, I didn't tell her anything."

Ignoring him, she puts on her coat. She grabs the doorknob, but Felix throws his hand against the door, pressing his weight onto it.

"Move."

"I can't let you leave like this, please stop for a second and talk to me."

She shakes her head. Tears are flowing down her cheeks now. "You know, I didn't even want to come tonight. I knew better. Yet, you pushed me into coming."

"I swear, I didn't know things would turn out this way. I would've never asked had I known, we could've just done something at your house, just the two of us."

"Are you being serious right now? Do you hear yourself?"

"What? What's wrong with what I'm saying?"

Many of the guests have deserted the dining table. They're peeking around the corner of the room, watching Felix and May.

"Did you think after Clint was gone that you could just step in and take his place?"

Felix scoffs. "Are *you* being serious right now? I'm not trying to take his place, I'm trying to get back to the way things were with you and me."

"Maybe that's your problem! You think things can pick up how they were before Clint came into our lives? Well, I'm sorry, but that's not going to happen. Things are *never* going to be the same. As much as you want to forget he was ever here, I can't, and quite frankly, I don't want to. I loved him. I will *always* love him. I care for you, but I will never care for you the way I did for him. I don't care what you do, how hard you try, you are nowhere near the man he was."

Felix slaps her. It was quick, but enough to leave her cheek red and stinging. She takes a half step back, sinking into the wall as much as she can.

"Oh my God, May I'm so sorry," Felix drops his hand and takes a step back, "I... I d-didn't mean to do that. I s-swear, it was an accident."

Without a word May darts out the door. She runs past the waiting carriages and horses, into the night. It's snowing heavily and the ground is slippery, but it doesn't slow her down. By the time she makes it home, her entire face is red and she's out of breath. Her chest burns with each breath. Her legs are too wobbly to make it up the stairs. She collapses onto the couch.

Christmas morning is surprisingly uneventful. She checks on the flock and feeds Star without interruption. The snow is still present, but the sun is shining. May is inside her house, making a list of things to keep and things to toss. Last night proved that she can no longer stay in Pine Valley and that it's time to set things into motion.

There's a soft knock at the door. She ignores it. Her closet is half empty now. Some of the clothes had needed to be thrown out anyway, they are old and riddled with holes. The red dress from the ball is still hanging. Her fingers caress the fabric. There are so many memories entangled into the dress. She sighs, pushing the hanger towards the "keep" section.

"You looked incredible in that dress," Felix says.

May jumps and spins around. "What are you doing in here? You shouldn't be here."

He's holding a bouquet of yellow carnations. His face is drooping with shame.

"I knocked, but you didn't come to the door... I figured you were still upset from last night."

"Upset is an understatement," she turns her back to him. "I guess I forgot to lock my door."

"Can we please talk about last night?"

"I would rather not. Last time we talked it went *so* well."

"How about I talk, and you listen?"

Felix walks over to the bed and sits down, holding the flowers in his lap. His finger nervously traces the pattern on a leaf. May pulls an old shirt from the closet and adds it to the discard pile.

"I didn't tell Becca, but I did tell someone," he casts his eyes to the ground, "I know I shouldn't have, but I tell my dad everything. I think he told Mark and then Mark told Becca, but May, I swear to God, I wouldn't have said anything had I known what was going to happen."

May doesn't respond. She brushes her fingertips over one of Clint's shirts. It's wrinkled, unwashed since the last time he wore it.

"I don't know why I slapped you. But God, I've never regretted anything more in my life than that. I've had so much stress and anger building up these past few months, I think it just boiled over and I snapped."

"Is this the first time you've snapped?"

"What?"

May turns around. "Are you saying you haven't snapped before?"

"Not towards you," he looks lost for words, "I mean, I'm sure I have, but nothing significant."

"Nothing significant? So, you're saying you never just snapped and killed someone?"

Felix drops the flowers. "I... I don't understand where you're coming from."

May walks to him and firmly presses her hands on his shoulders. She leans down so that they are eye level. His skin is paler than normal. A cold sweat embodies his entire body.

"I'm asking you if you've ever snapped and killed someone. If you could snap and hurt someone you *apparently* love, what's there to say you couldn't have snapped and killed someone you didn't care for? I mean if you really look at the evidence, I think you're the perfect suspect."

"I... I only killed him to protect you."

May releases her grip, taking a step back. The image of Felix stabbing Clint replays in her mind.

"Why... why would you?"

Felix stands up. He throws his hands behind his head and begins pacing. He briefly stops, attempting to catch his breath and gather his thoughts.

"I don't know where to begin. I wanted to tell you, I really did. My dad did such a good job with the cover-up, and he made me swear not to tell you."

"H-he was in on it too?"

Felix nods. "He helped me plan it, actually."

"I feel like I'm going to throw up."

Felix goes to her, offering his hand, but she pushes him away. She recoils into the corner, taking deep breaths. How could the two people responsible for Clint's murder also be those who helped May prepare for the funeral? It was Felix who made her dress and sewed Clint's outfit. It was Royce who made the arrangements with Mark and Morris, he was also the one who picked the flowers out from the festival.

"I was so angry after I found you. You know, I told you how bad he beat you that day? You were unconscious and bleeding, he left you out there to die. I was just going to shoot him and be done with it. I had my shotgun and everything, but my dad stopped me at the door."

"Stop."

He ignores her. "My dad and I went over there, together, and he talked him down while I retrieved the gun. Some words were exchanged, I don't remember his drunken slurs, but I shot him. I don't know if it was just once or if I shot him a few times, but I shot and killed him."

"Oh my God," May falls to her knees, "You're not talking about Clint."

"What?"

She covers her mouth with her hand. "You killed John. You and Royce murdered John and made it look like a suicide."

"Wait... you didn't know? Who did you think I was talking about?"

May doesn't say anything. She's still trying to process what he said. It was ruled a suicide. How could that have been covered up so easily? *This must've been what he meant when he said he'd seen a dead body before, it was John's.*

"Did you seriously think I had something to do with Clint's death?"

May looks up at him. "Can you blame me?"

"As a matter of fact, yeah, I can. How could you think I would even be capable of doing something like that?"

"... You just admitted to murdering John."

Felix stops pacing. He crumples to the ground, his back against the bed. He folds his hands in his lap. For the second time in his life, he's speechless. May scoots over next to him. She takes his hand and squeezes it. There's no anger or fear towards him for murdering John. Part of her has always been relieved he was gone, and it didn't matter how it happened. If he hadn't been killed, she might not be here today.

"I really wanted to tell you sooner, you have to believe me."

"I do... I'm sure this has been weighing heavily on you. You're not one for secrets."

"It has been eating away at me for years. Honestly, I'm sorry... for everything," he leans his head over onto her shoulder, "Where do we go from here?"

"I don't know."

He looks over at her pile of clothes. "What were you doing before I got here?"

"I'm going through the things I want to keep. Based on everything last night, I've decided that I'm going to leave. Clint and I were planning on leaving before he was murdered, and honestly, I don't see a point in sticking around."

"What? I know things were bad, but what about me? You would leave me?"

"Don't act so surprised, we've talked about this before. You have Royce, you're not alone. Besides, one day you're going to inherit the tailor shop and who knows, maybe Becca will finally wear you down. I don't think her affections for you will ever cease."

"What about my feelings for you? What if they don't go away?"

"I... I don't know what you want me to say. I can't give you what you want."

Felix turns to her. He places his hand against her cheek. He leans in, slowly. Suddenly, his lips are on hers. She doesn't fight him. He gently guides her onto her back. She watches him climb onto her. He pushes her hair behind her ear. *Clint used to do that.* He leans goes to kiss her again, but she puts her hand up. She feels nauseous.

"I'm sorry, I can't. It doesn't feel right."

Defeated, he slides off her.

"Do you think it would've made a difference had I told you sooner? About John?"

May sits up. "I would've thought of you differently, no doubt, but I can't say it would've changed anything. You've always been family to me."

He sighs. "Lucky me."

Chapter 15

"This is going to go better than Christmas Eve, right?" May asks.

It's the late afternoon of New Year's Eve. The sky is open and cloudless. Snow still covers the ground. The wind is strong and chilly, each gust cuts to the bone. May is standing outside the tailor shop. Star is hitched to the post in the back.

"I can assure you, this will be nothing like Christmas Eve," Felix says.

He leads her towards the lower level of the shop, where the kitchen is. The aroma of roast chicken floats in the air. Royce is in the kitchen. The table is prepared for three, with white plates, glasses, and a pair of silverware at each seat. A large bowl with a salad, plate of green beans and mashed potatoes sit at the center of the table.

"Good afternoon May, how are you?" Royce asks.

"I'm well, how are you?"

"Good, thank you. The chicken is almost ready, if you'd like to go ahead and take a seat. Felix, you can go ahead and bring the wine."

Felix takes May's coat before retreating down the hall to the wine closet. May sits down at the end of the table. She feels a little uneasy knowing it was probably Royce who spoke out about her pregnancy.

"How have things been? I know we didn't get to speak at the Christmas Eve banquet."

"They've been all right. Have you guys been busy?"

"Not more than usual for this time of year."

Royce brings over the chicken and sets it in between the other dishes. He removes his mitts and places them on the counter.

"I will say, you look much better than when I found you in that field."

May raises an eyebrow. "What?"

"You know," he places a carving knife by the chicken, "when I found you in that field, unconscious. It was a miracle you weren't injured."

Before May can respond, Felix walks back into the kitchen. He has two large bottles of red wine.

"I think this will be plenty, don't you?"

"Yes, I'd hope so," Royce takes one of the bottles. "Will you be drinking May?"

She shakes her head. "Just water."

Royce pulls the cork and begins pouring the wine into one of the glasses, while Felix takes May's glass and fills it with wa-ter. May watches Royce silently. *It could be a slip of words. The road verses a field... Maybe Felix misheard him. Maybe it was Star who was found on the road, and I was the one found in the field. It's plausible.* She pictures Royce approaching Clint that morning, knife tightly clenched in his hand, coming up from behind. Royce engaging him in small talk before he suddenly plunged the knife into him. Clint wouldn't have expected anything, he wouldn't have put up a fight, he wouldn't have known to.

Suddenly, Felix is pushing a full plate towards her. "May? Is this too much?"

"No," she takes the plate from him, "this is good, thank you."

Royce and Felix take a seat. Without hesitation, they both start eating. May takes a bite of the chicken.

"I don't want to talk shop on a holiday, but do you have any plans for the new year? I know things might be tougher with a child on the way, so we can renegotiate our contract as needed."

Felix elbows Royce abruptly and shakes his head sternly.

"What?" Royce asks.

"I haven't told anyone besides Felix yet, but I'm leaving. The sooner the better. I was hoping to meet with you about it after the first of the year. I know we previously spoke about you both taking over ownership of the flock, but if that's not doable I can sell them to a merchant."

Royce sits down his fork, taking in her words. Felix nervously takes a large gulp of wine. He pours himself another glass.

"You guys have been so good to me, especially after John... died. I can't thank you enough for everything."

"You really do owe my son a lot," Royce takes his fork up again, "It's a debt than can never be repaid."

Felix sighs. "Dad..."

"Excuse me?"

"Where would you be had he not found you in the woods? Dead? What about if he hadn't taken care of John? Clearly, that was something you were *never* supposed to find out about, but here we are today. My son has done nothing but take care of you, ever since you were both children, but you've barely given him a passing glance."

"What are you even talking about? I have never treated Felix poorly. I think it's safe to say that he's relied on me as much as I have on him."

"You were pretty quick to abandon him once Clint showed up, that's for sure. I thought maybe once he was gone, you'd wise up."

May's mouth drops. "You what?"

Felix looks over at Royce, his expression perplexed as well.

"You both know what I mean. I figured he wouldn't stick around."

"Are you sure that's what you meant? Clearly you both are experts at keeping secrets. Although, maybe you should work on getting your stories straight."

"Yes, I'm quite sure. I don't understand what you're getting at, but you best watch your tone when you're in my house."

"Dad..." Royce holds his hand up, silencing him.

"I think coming over here was a mistake."

"Yes, it's probably best if you go home Ms. Ferrothorn."

May stands up. Felix reaches for her hand, but she steps back. There is a pained look in his eyes. Without another word, May leaves. Star is patiently waiting for her. There's shouting and glass shattering from inside the tailor shop, but she ignores it. She climbs onto the horse and starts the solitary ride back to her farm.

There's banging on the front door, loud enough to wake someone even in the deepest of sleep. Her eyes shoot open. It's the middle of the night and darkness encapsulates May's bedroom. She reaches for her nightstand, fiddling until the drawer is open. Her hand grasps the pistol. The banging continues without pause. Slowly, she starts down the stairs. Her breaths are heavy. The white nightgown clings to her body. There's violent jiggling on the doorknob in unison with the knocks.

"May... May... open up, please. I need to talk to you." It's Felix.

Standing as far back as she can, she unlocks the door. He stops knocking and the door creeks open. May gasps and almost drops the gun. Felix is covered in blood. It's smeared on his face, stained on his shirt and dripping from his arms. There's a wild look in his eyes.

"F-Felix? W-what happened?"

He takes a step in and she takes two steps back. He closes the door behind him, leaving a bloody handprint. The gun is quivering in her hands.

"I killed my dad."

She covers her mouth with her free hand. "You... what?"

Felix crumples to the ground, tears are streaming down his cheeks. His hands lie defeated in his lap.

"I killed him."

"How? Why? Why would you do that?"

"After you left, we got into a huge fight. First it was just over how he treated you, and then it escalated from there. He admitted to everything. Your ewe... the dogs... the chickens, the fire, Clint... everything. He did it all. I don't know how it happened, I think I panicked... blacked out, really. One moment we were shouting at each other and then the next I was holding a bloodied knife in my hand."

May falls to her knees. "What about when he found me?"

"He was in the house, planting the knives. He saw you in Brian's room and panicked. Made some bullshit story up about finding you in the road."

"Why? W-why did he do all this?"

"For me. He knew how much I care about you, and he thought maybe, just maybe, this would bring us together."

She pictures Royce, for once not dressed in his usual attire, sneaking around her farm in the middle of the night. The knife hidden in his pocket as he lured her dogs away from the farm with a fresh cut of meat, twisting the knife into their hide when they weren't paying attention, followed by cornering a sleeping ewe, taking her and slitting her throat. He was just standing there, looming over the animal with a maddening look in his eyes as she bled out.

"That's really fucked up."

"I know, I'm sorry..."

May stands up and starts towards the stairs.

"Where are you going?"

"To change. We're going to have to go to Oak Ridge and tell Greg everything that happened."

"What," Felix hastily stands up, "No, we can't do that."

May turns around, one hand gripping the staircase. "We have to. We can leave John's death out of it, just start with everything that he did to me."

"Do you realize what will happen? We tell Greg and things get complicated, more complicated. Besides what I just told you, there's no proof of what he said. It's my word against my dead father's. I would look guilty. I would probably get convicted. Do you really want me locked up?"

Felix is no longer crying. He takes a step towards her. She looks at his bloodied arms. There are no defensive wounds. She takes a step back. *Something's not right.*

"What other options are there?"

"W-we can bury him. We could even do it somewhere on your property, or where we buried the chickens. We can say he left town. Sure, there could be some questions and rumors, but it would blow over, everything always blows over. Remember after John died?"

She takes another step. "And then what? After everyone accepts that he's gone?"

"We live our lives the way we were supposed to, *together*. I can help you raise this baby, I will be the father figure he or she needs. You don't have to leave anymore, it's safe. Clint's killer is dead."

May shakes her head. Her stomach is churning. What little she's eaten is fighting to crawl back up her throat.

"You and I both know that's a lie."

Suddenly, he's running at her. She turns to go up the stairs but doesn't make it far. He's on her. They fall to the bottom step. He climbs on top of her. His hands pinning her arms down, his face within inches of hers. The bitter wine stench seeps from his lips into her nostrils. He releases her arms and places his hands around her throat. She grabs for the gun, but it was lost in the struggle. She claws at his arms, but it's in vain. Slowly, her world goes black as she falls into unconsciousness.

May wakes up in a kitchen chair. Her gown is now stained with red patches of blood. Her arms and legs are bound with old rope. There's a stack of a dozen, untouched pancakes in the center of the table. Maple syrup sits in a pitcher. There's a place setting for two people, one on either side of the pancakes. The glass farthest from May is filled with wine, the closest holds water. The window curtains are closed, but there's no sun shining in. It's still night.

"F-Felix?" she calls out weakly. Her throat hurts.

He enters the room, still in his bloody clothes but his arms and face are now clean. He takes a seat across from her at the table.

"Good, you're awake."

"Why, did you tie me up?"

Felix rolls his eyes. "I wanted us to sit down and have a conversation, but I'm not stupid May. If you weren't tied up would you really be sitting here?"

"Yes."

Without a word, Felix pulls out her pistol and drops it on the table. *Dammit.* She looks away.

"I don't think it benefits you to be lying to me," he pulls two pancakes onto his plate. "We can stay here as long as we need to, hours, days, weeks, months, but I can't let you leave until you make a decision, one we can agree on."

"What if we can't come to an agreement?"

"Trust me, we will."

May watches his him eat. She hasn't eaten in hours, but she has no appetite. Looking at him gives her nausea. All this time, he was responsible. Her gut tried to tell her, but she didn't listen. Hell, she didn't want to listen. How can she accept that the one person she's known and cared for the longest is the same one who's destroyed her life? The same person she shared many nights with, spent her days with. Not to mention, she let him kiss her, twice. Her hands fiddle with the rope, but it's no use. Whilst Felix is not one to be considered farm savvy, he can still tie a formidable knot.

"Do you want any? I made enough for both of us."

She shakes her head. He shrugs his shoulders and continues eating, as if nothing is wrong. Her eyes are fixated on the gun.

"You can stare at it all you want, neither it nor you are going anywhere."

"Are you going to shoot me with it?"

He drops the fork. "God, no, what's the matter with *you*? Do you really think I could shoot you? Have you not been listening to me these past months? I love you, I would *never* hurt you."

"You already have. You've hurt me worse this past year than John ever did. You say you killed him to protect me, but what about yourself? Who is going to protect me from you?"

"I don't think you get it," he stands up and walks over to her, "You don't need to be protected from me."

He brings his face close to hers and she turns away. He grabs her chin and steers her so they are eye to eye.

"Everything I did, I did for you."

He leans in to kiss her and she spits in his face. Horrified, he stumbles back. She pulls her wrists as far apart as she can, hoping the rope will break or loosen, anything really. Again, she brings them in and pulls them apart. Felix is on his feet, standing above her. He slaps her, knocking her and the chair back. It hits the floor with a snap. The back breaking and loosening the rope's grip.

"Shit, May, why did you make me do that? I'm not trying to make this harder than it needs to be."

He sits the chair back up and goes to the kitchen sink. He runs his hand through his hair. Quietly, May slips a hand out the rope and grabs a knife from the table. She wants the gun, but it would be too noticeable. Her heart is pounding. Felix regains his composure and returns to his seat. He pushes his plate away from him.

"Even in death I can't compete with him."

"You never could. You're not half the man he was."

Felix approaches her again. He kneels so they are eye-level.

"He didn't see it coming. That morning, I mean. I guess you didn't tell him about our little kiss. Honestly, if anyone is to blame here, you should look at yourself. I mean really, look at yourself. Had he not been so trusting of me, he would probably still be here."

Tears are streaming down her cheeks. He's not wrong. She repeatedly assured Clint not to worry about him. It didn't matter how many times he expressed his concerns about Felix, she always brushed them off. Felix leans in and kisses her. His lips taste like maple syrup. He pulls away and wipes away a tear with his thumb.

"I'm sorry," she says.

"For what love?"

With all the strength she can muster, she plunges the knife into his neck. Felix stumbles back, grabbing at his neck. He pries the knife out and blood begins gushing from the wound. Quickly, she unties her legs. He grabs a napkin from the table and presses it into his neck. Within seconds it's soaked and limp with blood. She steps over him and picks up the gun.

"Please, h-help me... don't let me die like this."

She shakes her head, her cheeks still wet from tears, and points the gun at him. She cocks the gun and pulls the trigger. Maybe it's her ears, or maybe it's the adrenaline rushing, but it's silent as it launches a bullet into his chest. She pulls the trigger twice more, still, no sound. Felix lies helpless on the ground, unmoving, as a pool of his own blood surrounds him. He chokes as the blood puddles in his mouth. May walks to him and sits down on the floor next to him, her hand on his heaving chest. He takes her hand and squeezes it lightly, which is all he can do. He draws his last breath only a few minutes later.

"Please believe me when I say this... I never wanted to lose you too. I think I knew it early on, but I foolishly refused to accept that you did this. Felix, I always let you off easily. Maybe had I not, we wouldn't be here, not like this anyway."

After what feels like hours, she releases his hand and stands up. She pulls the thin afghan blanket from the couch and lays it over his body. She changes out of her gown and into a shirt, pants and lace-up shoes. She takes the sketch of Clint from the wall and sets it with the things she had packed to keep. By the time she has Star saddled and her donkey loaded with her items, the sun is in its early stages of rising. Everything is quiet, no wind, and no birds chattering in the distance.

May leads the horse and donkey to the front porch. She slowly walks up the steps, her legs quivering. She slides a letter under the door. The letter, addressed for whoever finds it, explains what they will find in the kitchen, why he's there, what happened to Royce, and circles back to Clint. After all, none of this would have happened had it not been for Clint. She pulls herself into the saddle and takes a deep breath. Star picks up a brisk walk and the donkey begrudgingly follows. With no destination in mind, she rides out of the gate to her farm. She doesn't take a parting glance, no, she doesn't want to remember it like this. The only memory worth having is when Clint was there, and the home was filled with his laughter and their love for one another.

Photo by Jo Haigwood

Kendal earned her MA in Creative Writing from Saint Leo University in 2024. She enjoys spending time with her dog and three cats, riding her horses, attending comic cons, and competing in barrel races.

www.kendalloudickson.com

Other Books by Kendal Lou Dickson

Lie to Me

Beautiful Disasters: A Short Story Collection

Learning to Trust Again: A Cat's Tale